create your o
erotic
fantasy

the classics professor

story by michael hemmingson
written by mary anne mohanraj

MELCHER
MEDIA

GOTHAM BOOKS

GOTHAM BOOKS
Published by Penguin Group (USA) Inc.
375 Hudson Street, New York, New York 10014, U.S.A.
Penguin Books Ltd., Registered Offices: 80 Strand, London WC2R 0RL, England
Penguin Books Australia Ltd., 250 Camberwell Road, Camberwell, Victoria 3124, Australia
Penguin Books Canada Ltd., 10 Alcorn Avenue, Toronto, Ontario M4V 3B2, Canada
Penguin Books (N.Z.) Ltd., Cnr Rosedale and Airborne Roads, Albany, Auckland 1310, New Zealand

Published by Gotham Books, a division of Penguin Group (USA) Inc.

First printing, June 2003
1 3 5 7 9 10 8 6 4 2

Copyright © Melcher Media, Inc., 2003
Cover photograph copyright © Michael Cardacino/Photonica

Gotham Books and the skyscraper logo are trademarks of Penguin Group (USA) Inc.

LIBRARY OF CONGRESS CATALOGING-IN-PUBLICATION DATA
is available.

ISBN 1-592-40031-0

Printed in the United States of America
Set in Garamond and Bodoni Book

PUBLISHER'S NOTE

a note to readers

This is not like other books. The individuals you encounter, the places you go, and the sexual risks you take are all entirely up to you. There is only one certainty: if you read this book over and over, you will have a wildly different, erotically charged experience each time.

As you make your way through the book, you will be presented with a series of choices at key moments. With each new decision made, you will be directed to a different page. Ever dream of attending every whim of a stern mistress? How about becoming a porn star? Or seducing a guileless coed? What you do next is entirely in your hands. If things don't turn out the way you imagined, simply turn back to the beginning and start all over again.

The choice—and the fantasy—are all yours.

New York City. Unfamiliar, unnerving even, but very exciting. You're walking down Broadway toward 116th Street. Everything looks strange to your unaccustomed eyes. You get a pang of homesickness for Chicago. You miss Chicago. No, you don't. You miss Sarah. If you close your eyes, you can imagine her here with you, holding your hand, happy to explore this city together. You open your eyes. You'll have to get used to being alone.

You continue walking downtown, passing bodegas, college students, Starbucks, an Ethiopian restaurant. You're on your way to a faculty party—the first of the school year. This is your first real academic job. You're only a lowly post-doc, and you have a lot of people to impress.

You pass a massive divinity school with high, fortresslike walls. As you get closer to the university, the streets become crowded with students. It's not a long walk from your place, down Broadway to the university, but it's more than a little surreal—bright yellow taxis dashing past, more people than you're used to, crowding through each intersection. And the buildings are tall, dingy. The streets are dirty, too; New York seems so much dirtier than Chicago.

Not that you mind; it adds to the aura of the place. Dirty, dangerous, intense. You feel like anything could happen here. You could find a hundred-dollar bill on the sidewalk, or you could get mugged for a quarter. You could meet a beautiful woman; you could take her to bed. You could even be a different man tomorrow. You well up with a tremendous sense of possibility. Anything could happen in New York City.

• PLEASE TURN TO PAGE 5.

"Five minutes sounds fine." You're cool, you're calm. Wendy nods approval at you, then turns away and disappears into the crowd. You pour yourself another cocktail and drink it slowly. Four minutes later, you walk quietly out the main doors and head up the stairs.

Her door is open; a dim light comes from a desk lamp inside. You step through and close the door behind you.

"So, what *would* you like to call me, Mark?" Wendy's leaning back against her desk, hands braced to either side of her, smiling. She looks oh-so-ready to be fucked. "Your slut? Your whore?"

You're startled—you hadn't expected her to go so far, so quickly. "Are those accurate?"

She shrugs minutely. "Well, I don't usually take money for it, so 'whore' probably isn't appropriate. But I'm not wearing panties, Mark. And I want your cock inside me. So 'slut' sounds pretty accurate. The question is, what can I call you? Are you willing to fuck me, right here, right now? Are you a slut, too? You kind of look like you might be."

You're not about to back down from *that* challenge, either. You walk forward, reach for her dress, gather it in your hands, and pull it up to her waist. She's not wearing underwear. Her cunt hair is black and silky; it looks damp at the bottom. She spreads her legs wider, bracing herself more firmly against the desk. Your cock throbs, hard, imprisoned in your pants. She reaches out and, with one deft hand, unbuckles your belt and unzips your pants so they fall to the ground. She pushes your boxers down, too, freeing your cock. Wendy reaches a hand up to her mouth, licks her fingers, slides them down to her cunt, wetting the lips, opening herself for you. Your hands curve around her bare ass, hold her steady as you position your cock, then you slide into her. Her tight channel engulfs your cock. You deliberately bite down on the inside of your cheek, the pain distracting you from coming right away.

She's the first woman you've had since you started dating Sarah six years ago. Her cunt squeezes rhythmically around your cock as you slide in and out of her. Sarah couldn't do that. Your fingers dig into the slut's ass as you pound into her, shoving her hard against the desk with each stroke. You're probably hurting her, but her legs are coming up, are wrapping around you, and she's arching up to meet you, silently fucking you in the dark room. Her heels dig into your bare ass, hard, and you want to punish her for that small pain; you fuck harder, faster, and now she's biting her lip. Her pale skin is flushing red, her body is shuddering, sending tiny ripples through her cunt, around your cock, and you're coming, you're spurting deep inside her. Her legs drop back to the floor. She whispers softly, "Slut." You pull out and put your pants back on.

Wendy stands up, and her dress slips back down, covering her hips, her thighs, her calves. She doesn't look like she's just been fucked.

"We should go back to the party," she says, patting her hair. "I wouldn't want anyone to miss us."

"Will we do this again?" You want to. You want to do it again right now. Months of disinterest, and suddenly your cock has woken up again. You find something compelling about Wendy Lake—maybe it's her direct, blunt approach. There's no pretense of emotion, affection. It's a relief.

"This exact same thing? No. We don't want to get tedious, do we? Come to my office hours tomorrow. We'll discuss it." She looks at you

4

for a moment, and an expression flits across her face, disappearing before you can identify it. What is she thinking? She turns away.

You fasten your pants, buckle your belt, open the door, and lead the way out. At the bottom of the stairs, Wendy pauses, leans over to whisper, "You're dripping down my thighs." Then she walks past you, into the roomful of people, full of light and cheerful conversation.

You take a quick breath and then join the party.

• PLEASE TURN TO PAGE 114

The campus feels so different from what you're accustomed to. The University of Chicago, where you did your graduate work, was a Gothic relic: low gray stone buildings, festooned with gargoyles and creeping ivy. The classics department stood at the corner of a quiet quadrangle of lawns, and the university itself was surrounded by Hyde Park, a protected academic suburb. Living in Hyde Park, you could forget the outside world existed—it was just you and your books, the old buildings, and the green grass. But here the architecture is neoclassical; redbrick buildings rise many stories high, with facades flat against the bustle of the street. This university doesn't hide from the city, and you won't be able to hide within its walls, however much you might like to. This is an utterly urban university, part of the city in a way the U of C never was. The school fits into its city perfectly.

The question is, can you fit in half as well?

You climb the steps of the classics building, open the door. Unexpectedly, you have butterflies in your stomach. You can hear the party—women's laughter, men's deep voices. You join them.

• PLEASE TURN TO PAGE 75.

Y ou respond the way she wants.

"Put them up me," you say. "Shove your fingers in there."

And she does. She's quick about it; there's no tenderness for your virgin asshole. At least she's lubed—it doesn't hurt, but it's a shock and an intrusion you're not ready for. Two fingers, and then three; she stretches your rectum and slides her digits in and out like pistons.

"Hang on a sec," you ask.

"You're going to take it," she says, "and you're going to like it."

"I don't like it."

"You will. Relax—these are fingers. Just think if it were a fat nine-inch cock. You can't imagine what sorts of things I've taken up my ass. Let go, Mark. Let my fingers fuck you."

Her mouth is right at your ear as her fingers pump in and out of you. You have to admit, in the privacy of your own head at least, that it's starting to feel good.

Wendy keeps talking. "Now, listen to me—this is the way it's going to be. You're mine, sweetheart. Your ass is mine, your dick is mine, that pretty mouth of yours is all mine. I'm going to keep them nice and busy. You can do your own work around my schedule—and when I want you, you're going to come, no matter what. Tell me you agree."

You nod. Your eyes are closed. You're trying to relax as Wendy pumps her fingers in and out of you with increased speed and intent, as shivers course through your body.

"Tell me," she demands.

"Yes," you say.

"I'll be here for you. I'll fuck you good and proper, as long as you're mine. As long as you do everything I say. Do you understand me?" Her hand moves even faster, and her other hand comes around to grip your cock, to jerk on it once, twice, sharply, and it hurts, but it feels good, too. So good that you can't help it, your balls are tightening, and you're starting to come, to squirt against the wooden door, and you say, "Oh, God. Oh, fuck, Wendy. Yes. I understand."

She lets go of you then and steps back. "Good. Come to my apartment tonight at nine. We'll have some more fun."

You nod, facing the door as you pull up your pants, buckle your belt. "I'll be there."

"And Mark—don't wear any underwear. Not tonight, not ever again, unless I tell you to. Understood?"

"Yes." Then you open the door, the door with your come drying on it, and walk out, heading across campus to the subway station at 116th Street. You don't understand what just happened—you can't seem to think straight. It's a short ride home, but you know it's going to feel like forever.

• PLEASE TURN TO PAGE 135.

Y ou decide to go for it.

"Sure, sell the tape."

Kimmie squeals and kisses you—then Rhonda kisses you, too, sealing the deal. Rick immediately goes to his desk and gets his checkbook, writing out a check for a thousand dollars. He also has some paperwork for you to sign. You sign, feeling a bit bemused by how fast all of this has gone. Rick insists on driving you to the station afterward; it's gotten very late, and since it takes close to two hours to get back to your apartment, it's no longer late by the time you get home, it's early the next day. You're going to have to shower and go straight to campus; you'll be exhausted and probably do a mediocre job teaching today, but there's nothing you can do about that now. After all, the sex was terrific, and it's all captured on film.

Before you shower, you feel the need to come just one more time. You stand in front of the bathroom mirror, watching yourself jerk off. Watching the muscles moving in your arm, watching your hand sliding up and down your thick, slick cock. You come all over the bathroom mirror, in long, thick spurts. You have to admit, you look pretty damn good.

Over the next few weeks, you get together with Kimmie half a dozen times to videotape sex at Rick and Rhonda's, traveling out to Long Island twice a week. By the third tiring train trip, you're making plans to buy a car sometime soon—that's going to be your first purchase with your porn-star money. A nicer apartment will come right after that.

When you arrive, Kimmie's always waiting at the door with a kiss; she's your main partner in the films. You're happy to see her, but there's a part of you that's disappointed, too. It's mostly curiosity. Curiosity and a particular kind of horniness. You've had a guy go down on you;

you've been one of two men fucking one woman. But you still haven't gone down on a guy yourself, or done anything else with a man. You don't know how you'd handle it, but you know you want to find out. Rick's always there, moving around with the camera, but sometimes you wish he'd put the camera down and dive right in.

Then comes the week when you arrive to find that both Kimmie and Rhonda have run out to the store to get some supplies, leaving you alone with Rick.

You don't even discuss it, and you don't make it upstairs to the bedroom. You just pull him into your arms and kiss him. It's strange, kissing a man, but not as strange as you'd expected. Rick's lips are thinner than a woman's, and the beard stubble on his face rasps lightly against your skin. It feels surprisingly good. You push Rick toward the living room couch while your hands unbutton his shirt and undo his pants. You lick a line down his hairy chest—the hair isn't particularly tasty, and you sort of miss having breasts there, but you're rewarded for it when you reach his groin. His cock is standing straight up, long and hard and eager—it jumps a little when you touch the tip of your tongue to it. Salty.

You lick him a few times, up and down, getting used to the strangeness of it all. And then you start sucking him in earnest, burying your face in his groin and really going at it. He smells strong, and he bucks eagerly against your face. You have to hold his hips down with your hands so you don't choke. It isn't long before he's coming, and you swallow it all, deep in your throat. You almost gag, but it's just a physical reaction. A moment's stillness calms the reflex, and then you're ready to flip him over and try shoving your cock up his ass—but the girls come home. You and Kimmie have a series currently in the works; it's time to make some money, so you'll have to save Rick's ass fucking for later.

Each session starts off the same; you scrutinize the best parts of the previous tapes, watching with your hand between Kimmie's legs and her hand between yours. The idea is to do something that you haven't taped before: a position, an angle, a scenario. Sometimes you and Kimmie become characters: a man and a wife; a brother and a sister; a college professor and a student.

It all really starts clicking when you come up with your great idea: costume dramas. You buy Roman togas for yourself and Kimmie. The next tape you do isn't just about the sex; you write a story line, too. You're not just Mark, you're Mark Antony, and she's the gorgeous, seductive Cleopatra. The black wig doesn't look quite right on her, and you briefly wish you could have Wendy Lake in the role. But the tape sells like hotcakes. You've discovered a niche market, and over the months that follow, you do more and more costume dramas.

You don't act just with Kimmie—Rick and Rhonda introduce you to different women. You do Romeo and Juliet with an agile French exchange student; you do Robin Hood and Maid Marian with a lithe brunette; you even write your own story about a weary traveler and a Japanese geisha, so you can work with a particularly gorgeous young Asian woman. Occasionally you fool around with a man, especially in the Greek stories. You make a terrific young Aristotle, and Rick isn't a bad Plato. When you fuck him up the ass, he whimpers beautifully. Who ever thought you'd be using all those hours of lonely library research for such a pleasurable purpose? The money gets better and better, and you're having a terrific time. The fucking is endless, and you think you're turning into a pretty decent actor. It's a good life.

Of course, academia gets more than a little neglected. All that weekend fucking doesn't leave a lot of time for research; you teach your classes conscientiously, but you don't do much else. Professor Benjamin gives you more than one warning, but you're having too much fun to care. Besides, you have faith that it'll all work out in the end. This feels right; it feels like what you're meant to do.

With all the fucking, you think you've gotten pretty good at sex. You look good on the tapes, anyway. You never did get that blow job from Wendy Lake—you figure you might give her another chance. She's still one of the most beautiful women you've ever seen, even if she is something of a cold fish, more into mind games than fucking. You leave her messages in the department, but she doesn't get back to you; she doesn't return your calls, either. And whenever you see her in the halls, she's always turning in to another room, stepping into an elevator, walking away. Clearly, she's avoiding you. Maybe it's because you didn't call her back right after her party, panting like a puppy dog with eagerness to be near her. You can't bring yourself to care much, so you stop leaving messages. She's attractive, but there are a hell of a lot of attractive, available women in the world, as you're discovering. And they all seem to want to suck your dick. What more could any guy ask for?

The end, when it comes, is sudden but not unexpected. Benjamin calls you into his office on a Tuesday afternoon in spring.

"Mark, I'm sorry, but we won't be able to renew your appointment for next year."

"I understand, Professor."

You're disappointed—it had been sort of nice, teaching the freshmen all about ancient Rome. You've developed a much deeper understanding of some of those ancient Romans than you ever had in grad school. But you have a much wider audience now; deep down, you're more relieved than anything else to be having this conversation.

Benjamin, on the other hand, looks genuinely disappointed. "Mark, what happened? When you arrived, you were so promising—did we fail you somehow? Did we neglect you or fail to provide enough guidance?"

You hate to crush the old guy, but it's probably better to be blunt. "Really, Professor, it was nothing you did. I think I just wasn't suited to academia in the end. I think I'll be happier in another field."

"Well, best of luck finding something. And if you're short of cash, do let me know; I imagine we can squeeze out a summer fellowship, at least."

"That's okay, Professor. I'll be fine—save the money for some poor soul who needs it, please. Thanks for everything." And you're shaking his hand, heading out the door, trying not to whistle. It wouldn't be appropriate.

As you walk down the hall, you pass Wendy Lake's office. You can't help glancing inside, and there she is, sitting at her desk, with a pair of glasses perched on her nose. She's still rather spectacular, and when she looks up and catches your eye, you grin at her and step inside.

"You heard I'm not being renewed." You look for a sign of affection, of regret—something to acknowledge what passed between you last fall. If it hadn't been for her, for her party, you wouldn't have what you have today. You owe her a lot.

"Yes." Nothing. Not a drop of emotion. The woman really is made of ice. Ah, well.

"Guess I won't be seeing much of you, then. Good-bye, Wendy Lake." You step back out the door, ready to walk away down the hall.

That's when she says, "Good-bye, Mark Antony." While you're still processing that, Professor Lake adds, "And by the way—nice work!"

And there's the smile, finally. Faintly condescending, perhaps, but also genuinely appreciative. It's nice to be appreciated. The famous Wendy Lake has watched your films! Now, that's an audience to be proud of. And you do let yourself whistle as you walk down the hall. There's a world of women to fuck, a mass of money to be made, and you're a young man with a very bright future ahead of him. Lights, camera, action!

THE END

Tuesday afternoon, you get off the A train at 190th Street and walk up to the Cloisters. It's at the top of a hill, surrounded by trees and shrubbery. Maybe Wendy plans to have sex outside. You've never had sex in public before, but there's something appealing about the idea—the risk of getting caught makes your heart pound faster, and there's a thrill in knowing someone might be watching and enjoying the view. You've never thought of yourself as an exhibitionist, but if Wendy wants to find some handy bushes, you'd be up for that. You don't see her outside the building, though. She's probably inside.

You pay the full ten dollars, wincing. But the place is worth it—a massive reproduction of five medieval cloisters, quadrangles enclosed by vaulted passageways. You pass one replicating an actual monk's garden, and you can't help feeling an academic thrill. The Latin manuscripts you specialize in are from the medieval period; the monks who copied them would have lived in cloisters exactly like these, walked through such gardens. Dandelion, nettle, wormwood. Cress, borage, primrose buds. Part of you wants to linger, but you have more urgent business to attend to. The Cloisters have been here a long time; they can wait.

You leave the monks behind and enter the chamber holding the seven unicorn tapestries. Wendy is there, alone in the gallery, gazing up at *The Unicorn in Captivity*. She's wearing a long, flowing dress in a rich burgundy-wine red, with sleeves that touch her wrists. With her hair falling straight down to the curve of her ass and her face tilted up in a shaft of sunlight, she looks like she's walked right out of a medieval painting. *La belle dame sans merci,* indeed.

You walk over to stand behind her.

Wendy says, without turning around, "I was always much more

interested in the ancient Greeks than in any of this medieval non-sense. All their notions about courtly love—sheer foolishness. But there's something about this particular tapestry that does appeal."

You consider the tapestry. You've seen it reproduced in so many books, but it's thrilling to see the original silk threads, the rich reds and golds, barely faded by the passage of centuries. The unicorn is tethered to a tree, constrained by a fence; the chain isn't secure, the fence is low enough to leap over, and he might escape. But his confinement seems like a happy one. He chooses to stay ensnared. You understand how he feels. You lean forward, whisper in her pale ear, "Maybe you like the idea of your men trapped, waiting to learn what you desire."

She chuckles softly. "That may be."

Wendy has a delightful laugh. You wonder if you can tease her into laughing more.

"Or maybe," you say, resting your hands on her shoulders for a moment, "it's the promise of true love that you secretly desire. Isn't that what those ripe, seed-laden pomegranates, dripping their juices onto his white flank, are supposed to symbolize? The triumph of fertility—isn't that what all women yearn for?"

"I doubt it." Her voice has turned cold again; the brief moment of friendly rapport is gone. She pulls away from your hands, turns, and starts walking down the passageway. "I've never found that being married does much for me."

You're startled. "You're married?" Is there an angry husband who's going to come after you? These days, you're probably strong enough to take him, but you hadn't planned on getting into any fistfights.

She shrugs. "We've been separated for years." You breathe a sigh of relief and follow her into a dark corner. "But let's not get prosaic with each other, shall we? That is not what I brought you here for."

"Why *did* you bring me here?" You're still trying to wrap your mind around the idea of Wendy as someone's wife. That makes you an adulterer, doesn't it?

"I brought you here to fuck me, of course. Now, please." And she's turning to face the wall, pulling apart two folds of her long skirt to reveal a slit, and through the slit, the white flesh of her ass.

Wendy wants you to fuck her right here? She's really pushing it. Why does she want to take such a big risk? The galleries have been practically deserted so far, and the corner is dark, but it's also open to the sky, and it would be easy for someone to turn the corner, to walk right into you. Isn't this taking it too far? Is the sex going to be worth the very real risk of getting caught?

• *If you unzip your pants and go at it,* PLEASE TURN TO PAGE 53.

• *If you don't want to risk getting caught,* PLEASE TURN TO PAGE 162.

There's a moment, a few days before Christmas, when you think she's about to leave you. Wendy is kneeling between your legs in the wide bed, looking down at your body. You're naked, spread-eagle, tied to the posts with silk scarves. She doesn't look aroused; she might even look a little bored. Your gut clenches. But the moment passes. Wendy suddenly laughs, for no good reason that you can tell, and then pounces on you, tickling you mercilessly. You have to fight not to scream as you squirm on the immense bed.

You don't say anything about it for a while, but at the close of the year, after several days when you've barely left her bed, you have to ask. It's very late, almost midnight. You were fucking for hours, and she's falling asleep in your arms.

"Wendy?"

"Yes, truffles?"

"A few days ago—when I was tied up—were you thinking of leaving me?" Your heart seems to stop as you wait for her answer.

She runs a hand down your chest. "I thought about it. We've been interviewing a new professor who'll be starting in the spring. I admit, I found him tempting." She pauses—you're still not breathing. "But then I realized that there was so much I haven't done with you yet, so much that I think you're capable of. I'm not tired of you yet, Mark."

You try to be content with that, though the *yet* worries you. But as the clock clicks over, from 12:00 to 12:01, the start of the New Year, Wendy adds sleepily, "I don't know if I ever will be." She chuckles. "Isn't that a funny one?"

As the new semester begins, she starts spending more time with you. Since she isn't teaching this spring—just researching and writing at home—you spend a lot of time together. She now throws dinner parties every Friday night. They start out ordinary enough—you, in some of your nice new clothes, partnering her, having a pleasant dinner with other couples: artists, writers, occasionally professors, though never any from your own school. Wendy is too kind to expose you to that particular humiliation.

As the weeks progress, the dinners turn more sexual. Wendy starts dressing you in tighter pants, thinner shirts. The other guests, responding to some unseen signal, begin dressing more provocatively as well. After dinner, people often make out—kissing and caressing in various rooms of the apartment. Never going quite to the point of full-out sex, but more and more teasing, until everyone's worked up into a delicious sexual frenzy. Afterward, you fuck Wendy for hours, and you're sure that the other couples are doing the same.

By that point, certain divisions have become clear—in each couple, there's one partner wearing less and less. By the first weekend of February, five dinners in, you're down to a pair of skintight black leather pants. Bare feet, bare chest. There are two other men similarly dressed—one in a leather collar, the other with silver chains at his throat and wrists. Three women, each one barely dressed. Two of them, Maggie and Yumiko, have often shared Wendy's bed with you; you hadn't realized that they belonged to someone else, that they were there on loan, as it were. Accompanying the six of you, the slaves, are the six masters and mistresses, fully dressed in formal evening attire—tuxedos and evening gowns. You've been initiated into a long-established circle of intimate friends.

It's so humiliating, but so sexy, too. The pants lace up the front, so that Wendy can easily unlace them and free your cock if she wants you to service her . . . or one of her friends. By the end of that night, you've been fondled by every mistress and master at the party. You haven't enjoyed it, but Wendy has. You can see it in her eyes, the pride she takes in you, in your muscled beauty, in their hands on your cock and balls, their desire for you, for her man. You put yourself aside and satisfy yourself with her pleasure. It's enough.

Then comes Valentine's Day, and the big party. Wendy has warned you about this one—she holds two big parties a year, on Halloween and Valentine's Day. They're much bigger parties than the weekly dinners; she isn't sure you're ready, but she's willing to test it if you are. You assure her you're ready—you don't want to miss this party, and you're sure you can take whatever she wants of you. Sex in public? Sex with other women, maybe even other men? You can take it. If it'll bring her satisfaction, you'll do whatever she wants.

The opening of the party goes smoothly enough. Many more people than you're used to—a larger crowd, all dressed, or undressed, to the nines. A black-and-white ball, so to speak, with the guests color-coded. Wendy is wearing a long black satin dress, plunging deep in front and back, almost to her waist. You're in white silk pants that fall low on your hips and lace on the sides from hip to ankle. A simple tug on each side would send them to the floor. You feel more than naked, somehow, as various eyes come to rest, speculatively, on those ties. No one reaches out, though—not without Wendy's permission.

You're serving canapés, taking quiet pleasure in your ability to balance a large silver tray on one hand while gracefully moving through the crowd and making conversation. Wendy is across the room, standing in the midst of a circle of black figures. Almost all the black-dressed crowd is over there, in fact. She catches your eye and tips her head, indicating that she wants you. You put down the tray and walk over.

Wendy smiles at you, beckons you into the circle. You step inside, feeling the pressure of their regard. All of their attention is fixed on you. She says, "Mark, sweetheart, we've been having a little bet. And I think you can help me win it."

"Yes, Wendy?" You're wary, but there is nothing you can do—just wait and see what she wants.

"We've been having a discussion about which of us has the best slave. And I think I have the best one, by far."

She smiles at you, and you can't help smiling back, feeling proud that she would describe you that way to her friends. You're close enough to smell her musky, sexy scent mingled with the heavy smell of her Creed perfume. But then she continues, "So I want you to tell them that, Mark. Tell these nice people how much you want me, how much you need me. Tell them how you and I ended up together; tell them how much you depend on me. Tell them how much you love me, Mark."

And there's a glint in her eyes, a triumphant smile on her lips—she knows that you love her, that you adore her, that you would do anything for her. And it's all true, but you don't want to say it out loud. You don't want to admit it in front of all these people—even if it would satisfy her, would make her happy. She won't make you do this, will she, if you really don't want to? If you ask her not to do this, will she let you off the hook? Do you trust her enough to risk finding out?

• *If you do as she says*, PLEASE TURN TO THE NEXT PAGE.

• *If you refuse*, PLEASE TURN TO PAGE 126.

Maybe you could trust her to let you pull back now—but maybe not. You aren't willing to take the risk of losing her. The room is well heated, but you feel chilled from the marrow of your bones. Maybe Wendy cares for you as much as you do for her. But you don't have the nerve to find out.

You chose to get into this mess, and now all your choices are done. All that's left for you is to do exactly what Wendy tells you to.

You close your eyes, take a deep breath, and start telling them the story. Tell them how you came home and found your girlfriend being fucked on the couch by a stranger. They like that detail—they step a little closer. You tell them how you came to New York and met Wendy Lake. You were enthralled by her. You grew addicted to her. You tell them how you lost your job and became her play toy, her willing pet. You tell them how you love the way she fucks you, the way she tells you what to do; you tell them how it gets your cock hard and your balls tight and ready.

Wendy reaches out and unlaces your pants while you talk, freeing your cock to demonstrate the point. It stands up straight and hard. She squeezes it, hard, hard enough to hurt. She pinches your nipples until they're red and sore. You keep talking with your eyes closed, enduring the humiliation, telling the crowd how much you love her, how much you need her—your lover, your mistress. Your very favorite professor.

THE END

Unfortunately, the end comes all too soon. The winter holidays pass pleasantly in an orgy of sex with Wendy, but there's a moment, near Christmas, when you see a faint trace of something that looks uncomfortably like boredom sliding across her face. It passes, but after that, she starts to call you less often. She seems busy elsewhere, and even when you are together, she doesn't seem all that interested.

You throw yourself at the gym: you work out for hours and hours on end, and then you shower, you dress in the clothes she gave you, the Hermès cologne she chose for you, and you wait. You wait by the phone, willing it to ring. By the time the spring semester starts, she's stopped calling you entirely. You go to the department, hoping to run into her. You never do, and it's not long before the look of pity on the secretary's face drives you away. She knows why you're lingering around Wendy's door. Everybody does.

It's not long before you hear that there's a new young professor in the department whom Wendy's spending a lot of time with. He's from Harvard and has a book contract already. She doesn't respond. In January, the checks stop coming, and you realize that you're finished with academia and finished with Wendy Lake. You could look for another mistress, but she wouldn't be Wendy, so there doesn't seem much point. You'll have to get a job, doing God knows what. Your life will continue somehow, but your New York adventure has reached . . .

THE END

Saturday morning you wake up early—much too early. You can't concentrate on work, even though you're supposed to be preparing to give a talk next week. Instead, you go to the gym, work out hard, until you're dripping with sweat. You push yourself until all your muscles feel like they're made of Jell-O—and then you suddenly start worrying that maybe you've pushed too hard, exhausted yourself. What if you get tired in the middle of fucking tonight? What if you can't perform up to Wendy's standards, especially if there's a crowd watching? Will she be embarrassed for bringing you to this party? Will she drop you like a hot potato?

When you arrive at Wendy's building, you're a bundle of tightly wound nerves. You lean against a stone lion that guards the courtyard, collecting yourself. You had considered chickening out, staying home. But you wouldn't have been able to live with yourself afterward if you hadn't even tried this. It's the sort of thing guys dream about, right? A relationship with a beautiful woman plus possibly extra sex with other women? How could you walk away from that?

The doorman smirks and waves you to the elevator. You take it up to the penthouse, and the elevator door opens to Wendy's hall. A man is waiting there with a clipboard in his hand.

"Name?"

You're startled—you'd expected Wendy to meet you. "Mark Matthews."

"Great, go ahead. You can leave your clothes in the guest bedroom; first door immediately on your left." He checks your name off the clipboard and motions you inside.

You walk in, wondering what you've gotten yourself into. That's quickly answered—you pass the bedroom door, walk into the vast living room, and realize you're the only person dressed. The room is a mass of people, all fairly attractive at first glance, and all of them buck naked. If you want to stay at this party, you'd better go back and strip. You don't see Wendy anywhere.

• *If you want to stay,* PLEASE TURN TO PAGE 31.

• *If you're going to pass on this shindig,* PLEASE TURN TO PAGE 163.

Y ou walk over to the patio door, where the girl is leaning against the glass, watching the crowd. Her eyes brighten when she sees you.

"Hey!"

"Hi. I didn't get a chance to introduce myself earlier. I'm Mark."

"Indira. Nice to meet you." She holds out a hand, the same one that was in her pussy a minute ago. You take it and shake it, slightly bemused. Her fingers are damp. "What do you do, Mark?"

"I'm a classics professor."

"Artist. Sheet metal and stained glass. Lots of solder." She gestures with her hands, sketching a shape in the air, vaguely curvy.

"That sounds interesting—I'd like to see your work sometime." It's a line, to be honest; you're not interested in her art. Modern art doesn't do much for you; you prefer work from the ancient and medieval worlds.

She tilts an eyebrow at you. Maybe she can tell that you aren't sincere. "I'd love to show you my etchings, but maybe later." Indira takes a step forward, into your personal space. Closer than is comfortable. "Right now I want you to kiss me, Professor Mark. And then have sex with me, the way you did with that blonde." She tilts her head up, smiling faintly.

That's why you're here, right? Three women in one week—it's bewildering, but you're not about to complain.

You bend down and kiss her; you have to bend quite a way. Indira comes up on tiptoes for the kiss, winding her arms around your neck. Her mouth tastes nice, sweet like vanilla and cinnamon. She has a gap between her front teeth. It makes you want to stick your tongue into it, and that makes you want to stick your cock somewhere else. This position is starting to make your neck hurt; you ease her down to the cold, sheet-covered floor, pushing away a nearby chair with one foot. She goes down smoothly, willingly, sliding beneath you.

Indira is a little tight to get into, but once your cock is finally lodged deep inside her, it feels incredible, like you're wearing a tight, silky glove. You start to fuck, and that's where you get your first surprise—she's loud. Really loud. She's moaning with the first thrust, and before long she's practically screaming. It makes you self-conscious with all these people here, and you put your mouth on hers, swallowing the screams. But she's too short for you to do that for long, not if you're going to keep fucking her, so you give up on trying to muffle the sound and let her go at it, concentrating on fucking, on thrusting in and out.

Partway through, she gives a small shove and rolls you over—then she's riding on top, doing the work, and all you have to do is raise your hips to meet her. Her breasts are hanging down, and you take them in your hands, pinching and squeezing the nipples. She likes that. You wet a thumb and move it down to rub her clit—it takes some coordination, but she really likes that. She gets even louder, and then she's coming, pulsing around your cock, coming hard, until she collapses against your chest. You aren't going to come yourself, not in that position, but it feels pretty good, and you're content to hold her for a minute. Then she's pushing herself up, smiling at you, and that's when she surprises you again. "I want you in my ass, please."

You nod and she slides off you, then goes over onto her hands and knees. It was less than an hour ago that Rhonda was in that exact position; this is all starting to feel unreal. Is it really you, Mark Matthews, doing this? The idea of fucking a woman's ass here, in front of all these people, is so far beyond anything you've ever contemplated doing in your life. Your pulse is beating fast, and you're sweating. To be honest, you're a bit scared, but you aren't about to back out. You move behind Indira but aren't sure what to do next. Your cock suddenly feels huge, way too big to fit into her tiny asshole. Maybe you should start with a finger.

You lick a finger, position it against her ass, press it in. She grunts, then pushes back at you. That's good, right? You slide it in and out a couple of times, then add another finger. Indira takes that, too, without any signs of trouble. Maybe this won't be so hard. You really want to get your cock in there; she seems ready. You pull your fingers out and use your other hand to get a lot of spit onto your cock, coating it. Then you position it against her asshole and start to push.

This isn't easy. She's incredibly tight—it's nothing like sliding into a pussy. It feels like you're trying to squeeze a tight ring over the head of your cock. And she's not moaning; she's making tiny grunting noises. But she's pushing back against you, so you push harder, farther in, until suddenly your entire cock head slides inside her ass. Indira whimpers—it sounds like you've hurt her, and you freeze for a second, not sure what to do. But then she's pushing back against you, and it seems to be okay, so you push farther in, slowly, farther and farther, until you're all the way in, buried to the hilt in this girl's ass.

You fuck her then, back and forth. It feels incredibly tight and hot—almost too tight but not quite. You put your hands on her hips, dig the fingers in, pulling her to meet you. Indira's so small, you can move her easily; she goes where you want her to. And she's moaning, grunting and moaning, deep, guttural sounds that almost sound like you're hurting her . . . but not quite. Or if you are hurting her, then she likes getting hurt. You're fucking fast, sliding in and out easily.

Sweat coats your bodies, and the pressure is building in your balls; you're getting ready to come, you're shoving her hard, pushing her down, down to the floor, fucking her flat against the floor, slamming into her small body, her tight ass, and the burning come shoots out of you, shoots deep into her ass, and you're coming and coming for what feels like a very long time.

Eventually, you pull out and collapse on the floor next to the girl. She rolls over, smiles at you.

"You okay?" You can't quite believe you didn't hurt her.

"I'm good." Indira curls up to you, rests her head against your chest.

"That's good." You stroke her hair absentmindedly, catching your breath.

"Hey, you want to cut out of here? A friend of mine's having a party tonight, too—a much more exciting one." She's licking your ear. Doesn't this girl get tired?

More exciting than this? This was pretty damn exciting. You just fucked a strange woman in the ass. You're still trying to wrap your mind around that one.

"There'll be some good stuff there. Stuff that'll really turn you on."

Drugs. She's talking about drugs. You've never had anything stronger than pot, and not so much of that. A few pot brownies in college; you've never even smoked a cigarette. Deep down, you've always been tempted by the idea of eating mushrooms or dropping acid—so many writers have talked about what it can do for you, how it can expand your brain. Maybe if you did more drugs, you would have more insights, you could become a better academic. And of course there's also the potential pleasure, the rush, the high. Your association with Wendy Lake is turning you into more and more of a sybarite—and why not? Is there anything wrong with pursuing pleasure? But you don't want to go too far. It's hard to be much of an academic if you're also a fucked-up druggie.

Indira's hand is gently caressing your balls, and while you're not about to come again anytime soon, it definitely feels good. Her other hand starts playing with one of your nipples, while her wet mouth is moving against your neck. You wouldn't mind spending more time with this girl.

When you glance over at Wendy, she's still going at it with the black man.

• *If you agree to go with Indira,* PLEASE TURN TO PAGE 82.

• *If you're going to pass,* PLEASE TURN TO PAGE 88.

It's an intriguing idea, but you're not ready to throw away your academic career quite yet. Maybe it'd never come out, but you're not willing to bet your future on that.

"I'm sorry, guys. I'm flattered, but I don't think I'm comfortable selling the tape."

Rhonda pouts, and Kimmie says, "Aww . . ." Rick looks disappointed, too, but manages a friendly shrug. "Oh, well—it couldn't hurt to ask. Still friends?"

"Of course." Part of you wants to ask for their copy of the tape, but that seems tacky somehow. It would imply that you don't trust them. So you chat a bit longer, say friendly good-byes with hugs and kisses all around, and then you head back to the city, a little worried and a lot tired. It's been a very strange weekend. You don't think you'll see these people again.

PLEASE TURN TO PAGE 194.

You go back down the hall to the bedroom door. When you open it, you discover a roomful of discarded clothes, on the bed, the chairs, the floor. You quickly take off your clothes and drop them into one of the bureau's empty drawers. Oddly enough, leaving your wallet and keys there makes you feel most naked. But it's not a bad feeling—it's embarrassing but also exciting. The apartment is pleasantly warm now that you're letting yourself feel this moment. All you have to do is walk into a crowd of naked strangers; the whole concept is surreal. All those women, all potentially available. If you think about it too long, you might end up overwhelmed. You should go out there, dive right in. But you can't seem to bring yourself to leave this room.

The door starts to open, and you feel a brief moment of panic—you're naked! And then Wendy Lake slips in. Unlike everyone else at the party, she's dressed, but not in much. She's wearing a sheer slip in some silky fabric that hangs to mid-thigh and hides nothing. You could lose yourself in the rounded shape of her breasts, the valley between them pointing down, across her gently curved belly, to her dark mound, her soft thighs.

You say, "You're not naked." Although somehow she looks more than naked. That fabric is an enticement to sex.

"Well, hello there, truffles. I am the lady of the house, no? I get to do whatever I want."

"I see." There doesn't seem much else to say.

Wendy looks you up and down; it's an oddly cold look, assessing. You have to fight the urge to slide a hand over your crotch. Apparently you pass muster; she finishes her assessment and nods sharply. "Come on, Mark. Rhonda's waiting."

You follow her out the door, down the hall, into the naked crowd.

"Rhonda, this is Mark. Mark, this is Rhonda."

Rhonda's tall, possibly taller than you, with long blond hair, a UV tan, and massive breasts. They must be silicone—they sit straight up at attention. She also has incredibly long legs; you've never seen legs that long. She has a pretty face and a shaved pussy. It's disconcerting, knowing so much about the body of a woman you haven't even said hello to yet.

"Hello, Rhonda."

"Hi, Mark. Want to fuck?"

Is this a trick question? You glance around the room and realize that while a fair number of people are walking around, chatting, there are also a fair number fucking, mostly on the floor. You can't see Wendy's furniture—white sheets have been tossed over everything, along with an immense number of pillows. Apparently that's all you need for a sex party—that and a well-stocked bar, where a near-naked bartender (dressed only in a black bow tie) is pouring drinks. There's no impediment to dropping to the floor and going at it.

Wendy is standing nearby, smiling faintly. What will she think of you if you turn this down? Why should you turn it down? This blonde is pretty hot. You'd like to fuck Wendy, but maybe she'll join in. Your cock is definitely responding, stiffening up. It's been a while since you've had sex with someone new, and there's no reason not to do this, right? Of course, it does mean Wendy might go off and have sex with somebody else . . . but then she'll probably do that anyway. At least this way, you'll be occupied for it.

"Sure. Be happy to." Your balls tighten, but you can't tell if it's from excitement or nervousness. It probably won't matter for long.

Rhonda steps forward and slides her arms around you, tilting her head down to kiss you. Her mouth is wet and mobile, her pert breasts press against your chest. Her hands slide down to cup your ass, digging in. In a few minutes of kissing, your cock has risen fully, and you're sliding down to the floor. You're kneeling, still kissing, and then she's pulling away and rolling over to rest on her hands and knees, her legs spread and her shaved cunt open and eager for you. You can see the juices glistening there, so you don't pause, you slide right in. Rhonda doesn't seem to expect, or want, much foreplay. She's kind of loose; you can't help thinking that she's probably been fucked a lot. You wonder if maybe you should have used a condom—but it's too late now.

You start pounding into Rhonda, and it feels great. Her cunt is wet silk sliding along your cock. She moans, she whimpers. You rest your hands on her plump ass, wrapping your fingers around her hips, pulling her back onto your cock. That feels good, but you want more body contact. You lean forward and pull her up, so you can gather her massive breasts into your hands. You fuck her like that for a while, both kneeling upright, fucking until the sweat is dripping off you. Then you lean forward, pushing her down again, going with her this time, your hands still squeezing her breasts, kneading her nipples. She's holding you both up; she's strong. You can concentrate on fucking, on the smooth pistoning motion that's making her shove back against you with each stroke, that's making her moan, louder and louder.

Rhonda's making guttural groans like something out of a porn flick, and you don't know if they're for real, but it doesn't matter. What matters is that she's making those sounds for you, and they turn you on, they make you want to fuck, faster and harder. You feel like you've been doing this forever. Your bodies are sliding together, sweaty, slick, and it's getting tough to get any purchase on her—this feels great, but you're not getting any closer to coming, and, God, you want to come. So you pull out, flip her over onto her back, and slide back in. And yes, this is what you wanted. Her back arching, her huge breasts pressed hard against your chest, her hips slamming up to meet yours, matching your rhythm, pushing you faster and faster until you both come and collapse, exhausted, flat against the floor.

Someone's been watching; you can feel the pressure of her regard. You pull out, roll off Rhonda, roll over. It isn't Wendy. You feel a stab of annoyance. She brought you to this, she pushed you at Rhonda. Wouldn't it have been polite to at least stick around and watch?

"Ooh, nice. Can I go next?" A tiny, dark-skinned girl stands above you; Indian, you think. Short, curly black hair, large, real breasts, sagging somewhat, slender hips. Young; she looks like a college freshman. Could be fun to fuck. It surprises you how quickly you've started evaluating naked women this way—fuckable or not? You've spent months with just Wendy, and you're starting to wonder if that was a mistake, sticking to one woman, and a difficult, controlling woman at that. Most of the women here seem pretty damn fuckable . . . and eager. You could definitely imagine fucking this one, but right now you can barely breathe, much less fuck.

Rhonda speaks up for you. "Maybe later, sweetie. Mark here needs a drink."

A massive glass of water would be very nice. Rhonda stands and reaches out a hand to you; you take it, and she pulls you up. She really is strong. The Indian woman shrugs and turns away politely enough, leaving you with Rhonda. "Besides," Rhonda says, "I want to introduce you to someone."

She leads you over to the bar. "Scotch okay? Wendy's always got great Scotch. And they say it gives you strength."

"Sure."

The bartender hands you a shot, and you gulp half of it down, the whiskey making a pool of fire in your belly. You sip the rest more cautiously; it's good. And then a man is coming up to stand next to you—tall, fit, naked. It's sort of like being in the locker room at the gym, but not really. This man is here to have sex, and that makes all the difference. You can't help glancing at his package—he's huge. He has a long, thick cock hanging like a heavy snake between his legs. The size of it fascinates you, but you force yourself to look away.

"Mark, this is my husband, Rick. I think he might like to fool around with you. Are you up for it?"

Well, you'd known this might happen when you came to this party, right? You hadn't spent much time thinking about it, but the possibility was there, lurking in the back of your brain. The only question is, what do you want to do about it?

• *If you're willing to explore fooling around with Rick,* PLEASE TURN TO PAGE 170.

• *If not,* PLEASE TURN TO PAGE 45.

Y ou smile at Rick awkwardly. You're still catching your breath. "It was good. Thanks." It *was* good. Now you know. You like having a man suck you off; you like having him kneeling there, at your feet, looking up at you and smiling. You tentatively reach out, rest a hand on Rick's naked shoulder. You'd always been curious about other guys; you'd just never had the opportunity to do anything about it. Now you have. You pat his shoulder once, gently, before taking your hand away. You like the idea of calling yourself bisexual—it takes a real man to admit to liking sex with other men, right? You enjoyed this; you want more. Maybe next time you'll be the one giving the blow job. You suddenly wonder if you'll be any good at it.

Rick is smiling broadly. "Glad you liked it, Mark. We're always happy to please." He's rising to his feet, glancing at Rhonda, who smiles and nods at him. "We were wondering, any chance you'd like to come by our house tomorrow for dinner? Our friend Kimmie will be there; I think you'd like her. And I think she'd like you. A lot."

• *If you accept their offer,* PLEASE TURN TO PAGE 128.

• *If you turn it down,* PLEASE TURN TO PAGE 173.

You decide not to call Wendy back. She was exciting, but you aren't willing to put up with that kind of game playing. All you want is a nice woman who likes having sex with you, only you. Is that so much to ask?

You don't see Wendy in the department the next day, so you don't need to say anything. You don't call her that night; she doesn't call you, either. You keep an eye out for her in the department the following day—you feel like you should say something. But you don't see her; it's as if she's disappeared. You leave your office frustrated, all of a sudden tired of New York.

• PLEASE TURN TO PAGE 134.

When you open your window Sunday morning, you quickly shut it again; there's a definite crispness in the air. Autumn is starting to turn into winter, and the shift of seasons makes you feel restless. Instead of settling down to work, you throw on a jacket and head outside. You walk down Broadway, not going anywhere in particular. Just walking. You pass the campus and keep heading downtown, not quite noticing the crowds around you.

Images keep flashing through your mind—mostly images of Wendy, but of other women, too. Rhonda. The Indian girl. A pair of blond twins at the party, being fucked on the floor, side by side. The longer you stay involved with Wendy Lake, the stranger your life seems to be getting. More and more sex, and in ways you never would have imagined in the old days when you were with Sarah. It's a fantasy come true; it's also surreal, disconcerting.

As you head into the theater district, the bright flashing neon assaults you. You can't help noticing the huge billboards advertising various shows—most of them romances, in one way or another. What you have now is intense, sexually exciting, but it definitely isn't a romance. After three months, Wendy continues to keep you at arm's length emotionally; she seems content with that arrangement. She's affectionate, friendly, but she doesn't make any pretense of loving you. And you don't love her.

There are so many couples here, walking around, buying theater tickets. You and Wendy could be one of those couples. You could go and buy a pair of tickets, invite her to a show. That's the sort of thing couples do, isn't it?

It's briefly tempting, but only briefly.

You head for the subway back uptown. As you walk, you take pleasure in all the attractive women on the streets; there are so many gorgeous women in New York. You might want romance someday, but not anytime soon, and not with Wendy Lake. You're having fun exploring the sexual side of life. You don't see any reason to change that.

• PLEASE TURN TO PAGE 194.

You hesitate, uncertain what her game is. You say, "Yes . . . Mistress." You feel silly saying it. But it seems appropriate somehow. Besides, this is a sex game. It's not serious.

She says, "Good. Now turn around. Hands flat against the door."

You comply. Wendy comes up behind you, her mouth at the back of your neck. "You smell good," she murmurs. She licks your earlobe. Her hands move down your back and then squeeze your ass. "And you have a nice, tight ass." She reaches around and unbuckles your belt; your pants fall down, bunching up around your ankles. She holds something in front of your face, a small rectangular tube of lubricant. It's between her forefinger and thumb, and she asks: "Have you ever been fucked in the ass?"

"No."

"Not even with fingers?"

"No," you reply.

"But you'll let me," she says.

"Is that what you want?" you ask.

"Yes," she whispers into your ear. Wendy opens the tube of lubricant and smears it on her fingers. The hand disappears from your face. She pulls your underwear down past your crotch. Her body is pressed against your back, her mouth is at your ear. "Tell me you want it, tell me you want to get finger-fucked, tell me you want them deep inside your ass."

- *If you follow her instructions*, TURN TO PAGE 6.

- *If you refuse*, TURN TO PAGE 160.

Fuck it." You grab your things, stuff them into a bag, hoist it over a shoulder.

"Don't forget your ticket," Wendy says, holding it out to you. "I'll change to a later flight."

You take the ticket from her hand without saying a word, stuff it in your pocket, and then walk out the door. You don't want to look at her again.

When you get outside, you wander the streets of Athens until you find an open hotel—one close to the shore and, more important, far away from Wendy. In the courtyard café, you order a bottle of ouzo, then sit there, downing shot after shot, trying to forget Wendy Lake. The pretty blond waitress, plump and cheerful, flirts with you in broken English. You ignore her at first—but by the third shot of ouzo, fucking her is starting to sound like a good idea. As a bonus, she looks absolutely nothing like Wendy.

You take the girl upstairs to your room, strip her of her clothes, and fuck her. You're not particularly gentle, but she doesn't seem to mind. You fuck her against the metal headboard of the bed, up against an open window, and the sea smell comes in, mixing with the girl's scent, the cries of ocean birds mingling with her moans and whimpers, and for a brief hour you can almost forget, almost let yourself be carried away.

But afterward, when the girl leaves, you're left alone with the bottle of ouzo and your memories of Wendy Lake.

THE END

Your dick feels heavy, and your tongue feels oddly thick as you say, "Okay. I'll do it."

Wendy hangs up, leaving you holding a dead receiver. You wonder briefly whether it's wise, obeying the woman like this. There's no good reason to think you can trust her. But that doesn't seem to matter—what matters is that she makes your heart beat faster. After the long months of numbness, Wendy is like a shot of adrenaline straight to the chest. You're getting addicted to this. To her.

You strip quickly, lace on shoes, and pull on your coat. It's only mid-September, and even at midnight, it's still too hot for a coat. You're grateful for a mostly empty subway car—one tired woman at the far end, falling asleep against the window; a few teenagers in hip-hop clothes, too busy flirting with one another to pay any attention to you. You keep the coat pulled tightly closed and stare at the dirty floor, thinking about your naked cock, pressing against the rough wool. Thinking about Wendy, naked, too, waiting for you with her fingers sliding in and out of her cunt, twisting on the bed, bringing herself off, over and over again. Your cock is painfully hard, and you tent your hands over your lap, thankful for the thickness of the coat. It seems much too long before the train finally reaches the right stop.

You walk quickly to her building, step inside, and nod briefly at the doorman, trying not to blush. His face is impassive tonight; you have no idea what he's thinking. Is it possible that he doesn't know? There's a part of you that wants him to know, wants everyone to know how crazy you're willing to be for her. That's part of the rush. She's waiting for you, naked, at the upstairs elevator door.

"Hello, Mark." There's a funny expression on her face—a mixture of satisfaction and something else. Affection, perhaps. You've been thinking about her the whole way; you're hard and ready for her. Wendy unbuttons the coat and nods approvingly at your erect cock. She says, "I see you've been a good boy." Then she pushes you down to the floor and climbs on top, fucking you in your heavy coat and sneakers.

Much later, she lets you take them off.

• PLEASE TURN TO PAGE 117.

You shake your head, stuff your wallet back in your pants. The boy shrugs and disappears into the crowd. You still feel shaken but steadier now. It was just a passing panic, a reaction to the drug's fading effects. You see Indira making her way toward you through the crowd; you stand up to meet her. She looks pretty, but nowhere near as beautiful as you remember her being. And when she comes up to you and reaches for a kiss, you feel more tired than anything else. She's a sweet kid, but not that interesting in the end. It must be almost dawn; what you want is to go home and go to bed. You're not a college kid anymore. It's time to go back to your real life.

You take Indira's chin in your hand, tilt her head up for one last kiss. Then you say, "I'm going to head out now; I've had a lot of fun tonight."

She smiles. "Me, too, Mark. Come to the gallery sometime."

"The gallery?" You're confused—you don't remember discussing a gallery. Everything from tonight is a little hazy, though.

Indira frowns slightly. "Wendy's gallery. She owns the one that shows my work—that's how we met. You haven't been there?"

You had no idea Wendy owned a gallery. There's still a lot about her you don't know, a lot you'd like to know. Maybe you shouldn't have left her party so quickly. "No, I haven't been there yet. Maybe I'll stop by sometime."

"Sounds good." Indira smiles again, then turns and disappears into the crowd.

• PLEASE TURN TO PAGE 38.

There are limits to experimentation. There are places where you aren't willing to go, and places where you don't want any other guys going, either.

"Rick, I'm sorry, but I'm not into guys."

"Hey, no biggie." He shrugs and smiles. "It was nice meeting you."

"See ya, Mark." Rhonda takes Rick's arm, and they leave you standing by the bar, an empty whiskey glass in your hand.

You wander from the living room gazing at Pan and his goat, at the enormous, erotic painting, to the dining room to the kitchen—the library door is closed, with a sign that says, "Library Is Off-Limits." You wander to the bedroom, where a massive puppy pile of thrashing bodies has developed on the bed. You contemplate joining it, but there are probably guys in there. If that's what being at a sex party takes, then maybe it's not the scene for you.

You go back to the living room, lean against a bookshelf, hang out a while longer. Not much else seems to be happening. To you, at least. Other people seem to have all sorts of things happening to them. Wendy is very occupied, up against a pillar with a big guy fucking the life out of her. Rick and Rhonda are fucking energetically under the big blue painting. The young Indian girl has apparently taken off. You watch for a while, but eventually that gets frustrating. You get dressed and go home, wondering if you're too straight for sex parties, if you're maybe even too straight for Wendy—wondering when you'll see her again.

• PLEASE TURN TO PAGE 151.

Y ou can't concentrate on the class. Screwing Wendy Lake has woken up your libido; you have to stop yourself from staring at your students, wondering what they'd be like in bed. There's a Japanese exchange student who wears her long hair in two braided pigtails; she tends to suck the end of one when she's nervous, which she almost always is. She's so shy that she won't look directly at you, even when she's answering your question. Would she be that shy if you were fucking her? Would she close her eyes, bite her lip— would her hands flutter against your chest like small, trapped birds, while you slid your cock into her tight pussy, fucking her endlessly on a long autumn afternoon . . . ?

You can't think about your students this way. There's no chance they'll hire you if they catch you fucking around with students. The graduate students are all of age, but the university has very clear policies on sexual harassment—no screwing any students you're actually teaching. Someone else's students are reasonably fair game, but you can't fixate on the ones in your class. Not even the blonde who insists on talking to you afterward and stands much too close, so that you can't help looking down her V-neck sweater at her firm young breasts.

It's three o'clock. Time to talk to the professor.

• PLEASE TURN TO PAGE 153.

"I don't think that would be a good idea." You're regretful, but firm. You're not about to jeopardize your career for random office sex, no matter how attractive the woman offering it is.

"You're not going to get a second invitation, you know." All the seduction has disappeared from Wendy Lake's voice—she's turned cold, slightly harsh.

"I'm sorry." What else can you say? That doesn't appear to be enough to satisfy her; she turns on her heel and stalks away through the crowd. Before long, she's back at the fireplace, comfortably ensconced in a new swarm of admirers. You repress a frustrated sigh. The last thing you need is another pushy, demanding woman in your life. Sarah was more than enough.

There's a quiet chuckle at your elbow. "Now, what could you have said to annoy dear Wendy? Is it possible the new professor actually turned our superstar down?"

When you turn, an attractive woman is standing at your elbow: shoulder-length chestnut hair, pale green eyes. She looks about your own age, twenty-seven or so, and a few inches shorter. She's smiling up at you, an infectious grin, and you can't help smiling back.

"Hi. I don't think we've met. I'm Mark Matthews." You're not sure what else you can say; no matter how much you've started to dislike Wendy Lake, it doesn't seem gentlemanly to admit that you turned her down.

"I know who you are, Mark. I'm Belinda Lundstrom."

Of course—you should have recognized her, since you've seen the photo on her Web page. You've been eager to meet her. She's the one Benjamin mentioned; she's tenure track and doing some very interesting work on the authorship of medieval Latin hymns. It's not far afield from your own specialty.

She doesn't look much like her photo—the girl in the picture had looked very young, almost like a college student. Belinda looks . . . not old, but not young, either. Sad, somehow. Still very attractive, though, with those wide eyes and full mouth, and a very nice body. You manage not to stare at her chest, but you can't help noticing that she appears to have quite large breasts under her white blouse. You shouldn't be thinking about that, though—it's Wendy Lake's fault, sending your mind into unaccustomed channels. Work: that's what you need to be focusing on.

"I've been wanting to meet you. I read an abstract of your work on ninth-century church music. Do you spend a lot of time in France?"

Belinda smiles, clearly pleased. She's quick and witty—and her engagement with her work gets you excited about your own writing. Before long, you're deep in conversation, the first academic conversation you've had in a long time that actually interests you. There's something about her that you find very appealing; maybe it's the hint of sadness, the vulnerability it implies. When the party winds down, you don't want to stop talking. She seems to like you, too; she's leaning forward, and your heads are almost touching. You've had a few drinks—maybe that's what makes you bold enough to ask, as you're putting on your jackets, "Belinda, would you like to go for coffee sometime?"

She hesitates. Damn, maybe she's married. You didn't even think to ask. You glance down at her finger; no ring, but there's a thin tan line where a ring should have been. Divorced? But before you can ask, she says, "Sure. I'd like that."

"Tomorrow? Around three?" Are you being too eager? It's been many years since you asked a woman out.

"That'd be fine. I'll be here. Come pick me up in my office."

Apparently not too eager. And a woman who works on a Sunday—now, that's the kind of woman you should be with. She's not likely to complain that you work too much.

"Terrific. I'll see you then." You walk out the door with her, turn to go in your separate directions home. Something makes you look back, watch her walk away down the street. Belinda is attractive from the back, too—a lush ass in a short gray skirt, and slender legs. She seems to be walking with a slight limp; maybe you kept her talking too long on her heels. You go home to your tiny apartment, whistling. You've successfully asked a woman out—so there, Sarah. You can do fine without her.

→

You pick Belinda up on Sunday. She's wearing gray again, a soft dress that emphasizes her curvy shape. The weather is unexpectedly mild—a beautiful Indian-summer day. She steers you to a tiny cafe with a red and white awning, a Hungarian pastry shop, where you end up placing an order for coffee and a decadent Sacher torte with a waitress who has trouble understanding your order. It doesn't matter—you don't really care about the food. You care about sitting at a comfortable wooden table with beautiful Belinda, in the warm, open air, enjoying the view of St. John the Divine. It's almost, you think, like being in Paris. How long has it been since you've been so comfortable, relaxing and spending time with an attractive woman? You can't remember ever being this content.

The conversation is even better this time; she's stiff at first, but once she relaxes, she's funny. Belinda's wry comments about her colleagues make you laugh. She even puns in classical Latin. And instead of sticking to work, you end up talking about all sorts of things—the department, the university, the city. Music. She's passionate about medieval music: she plays alto in a recorder consort. You even discuss sports; she's a Red Sox fan, as it turns out. You can't believe how much you have in common—a lot more than you ever had with Sarah. Eventually, you ask Belinda about that missing ring. You're itching to know.

"So, divorced?" You nod toward the finger with the tan line. She glances down and flushes.

"No, actually. Widowed." Her lively manner has disappeared; she bites her lip, and small lines appear on her forehead.

"You're too young to be a widow!" You have a definite mental image of widows, and they're old, older than your grandmother, and dressed all in black.

"Nonetheless. Joseph and I were married two years; we were in grad school together. He died last year—car accident." When you'd been talking about school and music and sports, she'd looked like a college student again. Young, laughing. Now she's somber, looking her age. You feel obscurely guilty.

"I'm so sorry." You reach out impulsively, take her hands in yours. It's the first contact you've had with her . . . and it's electric. You feel like there are sparks running through your whole body. You want to pull her into your arms and kiss her—but that would be utterly inappropriate. You've known Belinda for only a day, and she's a colleague. You're busy stifling that impulse when she says, "Mark? Do you like me?" She's looking down at her coffee, biting her lip.

"Of course I like you." You like her a lot.

Belinda looks up. "Do you want to come back to my place?"

Is she saying what you think she's saying? Her hands are shaking in yours. You squeeze them gently. It looks like she is. If you go to her place, you'll probably end up having sex. You'd known sex would be a possible outcome with Belinda, but you hadn't expected it to come up so quickly. Are you ready for this, with her, so soon?

• *If you say yes,* PLEASE TURN TO PAGE 186.

• *If you say no,* PLEASE TURN TO PAGE 104.

Your mouth twists. "That's disgusting. I can't do it, Wendy— ask me to do something else."

Wendy's smile disappears, and her eyes turn cold. "I wasn't asking. And you've forgotten our agreement. I'm afraid you'll have to leave." She's still naked, a beautiful woman in her bed, but she looks totally unapproachable. You feel a flash of anger, but what are you going to do with it? You're not the sort of guy who'd force himself on a woman.

You get out of the bed, pull your clothes on. "So, that's it?" You're pleased that your voice is utterly calm. If she wants to be cold and distant, you can do that.

Wendy shrugs. "I'm not interested in a guy who can't satisfy me—and who can't keep up with me."

So she wants to get mean? "Fine. I'm not interested in a bitch who wants to play head games."

You walk out the door quickly. It was a mistake getting involved with a woman at all. Wendy Lake might be smart and beautiful and rich—but she's still a woman, which means she's still a hazard to your life, your career, pure trouble waiting to happen.

You learned that lesson with Sarah; you just needed a reminder. You're not going to bother with women again. Not for a long time, anyway. You need to concentrate on you for a change, instead of on trying to please demanding women. You and your books: that's all you need. And if you feel physical urges, you can always find a hooker. It's New York, after all. There are plenty of them around.

THE END

You're nervous, but you're also turned on by the risk. You feel dizzy; your mouth is dry. You unzip your pants, pull out your half-hard cock, step forward, and push it through the slit in the fabric of her skirt. She spreads her legs, bracing herself against the rough stone wall. Some of those stones may have come from medieval England—you find the thought oddly exciting. The skin of her ass is incredibly soft; your cock gets hard, and the tip of it finds her wet pussy. Maybe she finds this exciting, too, fucking among the remains of antiquity.

You slide into her—a few quick strokes, shoving her up against the wall. You lean forward, pressing you both as close to the wall, and its shadows, as you can. You brace your hands against the stones as you fuck her; they're cold, damp, smeared with dirt. But her cunt is hot around your cock, and as you fuck her, Wendy starts to whimper. You don't want anyone to hear you. You cover her mouth with your dirty hand, pressing down, muffling the sounds. You fuck her hard, almost lifting her off the ground. This time, you hold off until you can feel her trembling, until shivers are racing through her and she's biting your hand, moaning loud enough that your heart starts pounding—someone is sure to hear this! You finish quickly then— if she hasn't actually come yet, too bad for her. A few more rough thrusts and you're done, spurting into her, pulling out, zipping up your pants, with your heart still thumping loudly. The folds of her dress fall back into place, concealing.

A heavyset guard comes down the passageway right as she turns around. "Everything okay here?" His thick brows are drawn together as he peers at you both suspiciously.

"Fine," she says, looking cool and calm—but with smears of dirt on her mouth and all down the front of her dark red dress.

54

The guard shrugs and walks away.

Wendy turns to you and smiles. It's an odd smile—satisfied, but not particularly friendly. "Good timing. Want more?"

"Sure." Of course you want more, but maybe not right now, or right here. You don't want to end up in jail. You wait, curious to see what she'll suggest next. Going back to her place again? You can think of all sorts of things you'd like to do to her there, if she'll let you.

"I'll call you." She turns and walks down the long stone hallway without giving you an opportunity to say anything more. So you stand there, watching her ass move under the folds of the red dress, hoping for one last glimpse of pale flesh. But her dress covers everything.

• PLEASE TURN TO PAGE 167.

"Okay," you say. "Fine." Then you roll over on top of her, kissing her, sticking your tongue in her mouth, shoving her thighs apart with your legs, and pushing your cock into her cunt. You're being blatantly possessive, demanding, and she lets you, but you can't get rid of the feeling that she's amused by the whole show. You tell yourself you don't care—as long as you can slide your hard cock in and out of that silky, tight cunt. As long as Wendy lets you stay with her, lets you keep fucking her. The thought of leaving her makes your throat and chest feel tight. The thought of her leaving you is worse.

Afterward, she kisses your cheek reassuringly. She kisses your lips. She climbs up the bed, kneeling over your face, and you lick and suck, you eat her out until your tongue feels like it's going to fall off. Wendy comes again and again. Afterward, she sends you home as usual—but she gives you a small pat on the cheek before she sends you away. It's not any kind of promise, but somehow it makes you feel better.

As the weeks pass, September turning to October, she asks for more from you. She likes you blindfolded, likes to rub ice cubes across your naked body, to drip hot candle wax on your skin. She likes to tie you down with blue silk scarves before she fucks you. One night, she asks you to dance for her, like a stripper. You start out slow, uncertain, unbuttoning your shirt, button by button. Wendy directs the show; when you go too fast for her, she makes you go back, button your shirt again, do it over. She puts on music, and you find it's not so hard, moving to the beat.

You are humiliated but aroused, too, knowing that Wendy is watching you, enjoying the sight of your body as it's slowly revealed, piece by piece. All the hours at the gym seem worthwhile now, with first her eyes, and later her hands, moving hungrily over your skin, the muscles underneath. Wendy whispers in your ear, "You're beautiful, Mark. Just beautiful." You're flattered, though disconcerted, too. No one has ever called you beautiful before.

I t's not all sex.

On a Thursday in late October, Wendy gets a call from her agent—she's contracted for another book, a six-figure advance. You tell her congratulations, but there's a twist of envy in you—you know that no matter how hard you work, you'll never have that kind of success. You try not to think about it.

Wendy starts spending most of her free time doing research for the book and outlining arguments—planning to draft it in the spring, a semester when she won't be teaching. She has a library at the far end of the apartment, and a large, comfortable leather chair. She likes to sit there, outlining chapters, with a stack of books piled up beside her and a glass of Scotch perched on the arm of the chair.

You sit at her feet, reading while she works. It makes you feel warm and safe; leaning against her knee, with her hand ruffling your hair, you feel happier than you've felt since you were a child. She has an amazing collection: old manuscripts, first editions. Some of these books should be in university collections.

One afternoon, you look up from a copy of Hereford's *Mappa Mundi* and ask her, "How much did *this* cost?"

Wendy shrugs without looking up from her notebook, her pen moving quickly over the paper. "I don't know. It was a gift."

Some of Wendy's lovers offer her far more than you can. She could easily grow tired of you. She seems to care for you—she's become more affectionate as the weeks have passed, freer with kisses and caresses. But she hasn't made you any promises. You have no guarantees that she'll continue to want you around. You read more, and you read in her field instead of yours, so that you can offer clever insights when she reads you paragraphs of her new book. You rub her feet with lotion; you bring her fresh drinks. Wendy seems happy, so you're happy, though it's a fragile, tentative happiness.

Then she sends you away.

It's Halloween. The campus is dotted sporadically with students in costume and the occasional professor. Everyone's passing out candy, and you've had too much. You're quite queasy. You're in your office, resting before office hours start. The phone rings—it's Wendy. She never calls you at the office.

"Mark, meet me at the apartment." She means her apartment, not yours. Never yours. "Wait for me in the bedroom."

You cancel your office hours, leaving a note for the scheduled students. When you get to Wendy's apartment, the doorman gives you a big wink. "Big night tonight!" You nod agreement, bewildered. You don't know what he's talking about. You go upstairs, to her bedroom, and wait.

Wendy comes in, pulling off her dress as she walks through the door. She looks unusually flustered—she's talking, too, though it's hard to make out the words through the fabric around her head. ". . . completely lost track of time—I can't believe it's Halloween already!" Then the dress is off, and she's opening a closet door that you've never seen her open before, pulling out a rack of what look like costumes. As she starts shuffling through them, you realize that they aren't Halloween costumes—they're sexual costumes. There's a French-maid outfit, a tiny red vinyl hooker dress, a fish-net bodysuit, a long black dress with a slit that looks like it goes all the way up to the waist. You imagine Wendy in the outfits; your cock stirs, and you shift on the bed. Wendy turns and looks at you then, one hand resting on her bare hip, considering.

"Mark, I don't think this is going to work." She says it slowly, as if she's just decided this.

"What?" Somehow you don't quite trust her sincerity. You wouldn't be surprised if she brought you here so you could be turned on and then disappointed. It wouldn't be the first time she's teased you like that.

"I thought I could get you up to speed quickly, but I don't think you're prepared for tonight. You'd better go home. I'll call you soon." And then she's turning back to the outfits, relaxed in her certainty that you will leave quietly, as instructed.

She's right, of course. You get up, gather your coat, and go home. You know she won't even tell you what this was all about. You try not to look at the doorman on your way out.

You spend Halloween waiting for it to be over, trying not to think about what's happening at Wendy's apartment, about who might be there, fucking her. You almost expect her to call the next day and tell you she's met someone else who'll be taking all of her time and attention, that she doesn't have room in her life for you anymore. You brace for that call; you tell yourself you'll be fine—you'll throw yourself into your work the way you did when you lost Sarah. You don't believe yourself.

Wendy calls the next day, but only to invite you over, as usual. It's as if Halloween never happened.

You're still teaching, but you've given up any pretense of doing research. It's not Wendy's fault—she doesn't demand so much of your time that you couldn't keep doing your work. You just can't bring yourself to care.

When the time comes for you to give a seminar presentation in late November, on the research you were supposedly doing all semester, you offer up a barely thought-out rehash of your dissertation. Twenty minutes into the talk, people start slipping out the back. By the end, only a few diehards remain in their chairs, among them Professor Benjamin, who doesn't look surprised at all—just saddened. You're sorry you've disappointed the old man, but he could never understand how things have changed for you.

After the seminar, you go back to Wendy's apartment, and she asks you to fuck her up the ass, her body pressed naked against one of her broad windows, open to the city's view. How much can you care about the ancient world when the modern one holds Professor Wendy Lake?

In the first week of December, Benjamin calls you into his office. He tells you that the department is unhappy with your work and they'd prefer it if you didn't come back after the winter holidays. You tell him you understand—you do. You wouldn't have hired you back, either.

That night, after sex, you tell Wendy you've lost your job.

Wendy frowns at you—not angrily. More . . . consideringly. "Well, I probably should have anticipated this. How much are you paying in rent, Mark?"

"Ten fifty. And I have student-loan payments." It's embarrassing to admit—you're not sure how much her place costs, but it must be at least a few thousand a month.

She shrugs. "I can manage that, plus something for groceries. Don't worry about it, sweetheart." She leans over and kisses your cheek. "Now, come over here and suck my clit, okay?"

So, there it is on the table—you can keep being Wendy's sex slave, and she'll pay your expenses, as long as they're not too expensive. You wouldn't have to work at all; you could sleep away the day and have sex all night. It's every man's dream—or is it?

You're not sure how you've gotten to this point, where you're seriously considering letting a woman take care of you. Of course, it's not just any woman—it's Wendy. That makes all the difference. You're sliding perilously close to being obsessed with her—with her body, with the way she treats you, with the way she tells you what to do. You want Wendy; you need her. If you let her pay your rent, then you'll really need her.

If you're ever going to walk away from her, now is the time.

• *If you let Wendy pay for your living expenses,* PLEASE TURN TO PAGE 197.

• *If you refuse her generous offer,* PLEASE TURN TO PAGE 210.

"Belinda? It's Mark. Can I come over?"

She says yes. You take the subway there. When she opens the door, you pull her into a quick, reassuring hug before stepping into the apartment, closing the door behind you.

Belinda is nervous. You can see it in her eyes, her stance. She's in that ever-present gray again: slacks and a sweater this time. She wears it like armor. You suddenly realize that two years later, she's still in mourning—though whether it's for her dead husband or for herself, it's impossible to tell. She's standing particularly upright; you can't detect from looking at her that there's anything wrong with her body at all.

Maybe there isn't. Not really.

"Look, Belinda—I don't know if I'll be able to cope with this. I can't promise that. But I'd like to try."

She's still frozen for a minute, as if she were expecting something else. Of course she was. But then she relaxes and smiles at you, and you can't believe how amazing she looks. It's as if Belinda has been holding something back, tense and braced for pain, the entire time she's known you. She doesn't say anything, merely steps forward and kisses you. Your arms curve around her, pulling her close. You kiss her, first lips against lips, as gently as you can. But then her kiss grows fiercer, her lips pressing hard against yours, her mouth opening, and your breath comes faster, your pulse is pounding, and you kiss back, hard, your mouth opening, your tongue tangling with hers. When you finally break away, you're both short of breath, dizzy. Belinda takes your hand and leads you, shyly, to her bedroom.

You take off her clothes, slowly. All of them. Then your own. You try not to stare—you're curious, but you don't want to make her uncomfortable. You can't see anything different in her shape, not anything obvious. Her skin is marked, though. In the bright sunlight coming through the window, you can see scars—not many, but a few. Dark, ridged lines on her hips and her thighs. Somehow, they make you want to kiss them. So you do. You lie down with her on the bed, and when she starts to reach for your hard cock, you stop her. You take her wrists in your hands and pin them down to the bed on either side of her body. You kiss her lips again, and then start kissing your way down her body, slowly, taking great care not to rest your weight on her at any point. You kiss her chin, her collarbone, the valley between her breasts. You linger at her stomach; you lick circles around her navel. You slide down and down, skimming over her hips until you reach her mound—then you breathe, as lightly as you can. Belinda shivers and arches. It's beautiful, that arch.

You take a long time, licking her pussy lips, tracing patterns there. Her scent is very faint, barely there. A hint of salt, of sea. Everything about Belinda is hidden, secret—you must lick her for a long time before her clit emerges, shy and delicate, yet eager in its own way. You don't use your fingers—not this time. There'll be plenty of time later to find out exactly how far you can go while still giving her pleasure. For now, you're entirely gentle, touching and tasting, licking and nibbling, as her shivers are joined by panting breaths, by whimpers. When she's twisting, sweating in the sheets, that's when you start sucking, your hands reaching up to her breasts, squeezing the nipples, and when she comes, she comes hard, moaning, shuddering against you.

You crawl back up again then, still hard, still horny, but in some sense, entirely satisfied. For right now, you're content to hold Belinda, letting her head rest against your shoulder, feeling the total relaxation in her body. You did that. You're proud of it.

It isn't all that easy. The next few days go smoothly, but then there's the night when you get a little too turned on, too eager. You're embracing Belinda, kissing her neck, her collarbone, your naked body pressed up against hers, your cock hard against the entrance to her wet pussy, and it seems so natural to start sliding in there. It feels so good—and it's only when you open your eyes and see Belinda biting her lip, her face drawn and taut, that you realize what you're doing and jerk away, breathing hard, trying to quiet your body down. When you're calm again, you touch Belinda's cheek in apology and then slide down to take her pussy in your mouth, trying to make up with pleasure for any small pain you might have caused her.

So, sometimes you forget. Sometimes you get frustrated. But the rest of the time is so good—having sex with her, talking to her, making her laugh—that you have plenty of incentive to stay with it, to try to do better. And as the weeks pass, September to October to November, you grow very fond of Belinda Lundstrom.

You take her to the park, to dinner, to Broadway shows. Belinda is a delightful companion—funny and smart and incredibly sweet. By the time December rolls around, you realize that you could stay with this woman for a long time—maybe for the rest of your life. You start looking forward to the future, to semesters of working together, to summers traveling abroad for conferences, and, of course, to lots and lots of inventive sex. You're even planning to convince Belinda to wear clothes with some color to them. You wonder what she'd look like in green, with that dark brown hair curling around her shoulders—like a slender tree in springtime, bending in the wind.

You're not sure where this relationship will end up, but so far, you're enjoying the way it's going.

THE END

The phone rings, two, three times. She isn't home. Your chest feels strange—cold and tight. That makes it easier. You leave a message on her machine, telling her you're sorry, but this isn't the kind of relationship you're looking for. You say you respect her immensely and look forward to working together. You pause, feeling like you should say something else, but you can't think of anything else. So you hang up the phone. You feel like a schmuck, but you know yourself well enough to know that it's better this way. It would have been too hard, never having intercourse again. There would have come a day when you pushed her, or when you left her, or when you cheated on her with someone else, someone who could have normal sex. If you tried to date Belinda, you'd hurt her more in the end.

The weeks that follow aren't easy. Wendy Lake occasionally glares at you in the hallways of the department. Belinda avoids you. But your work is going well, and you manage to put your troubles with women aside. You finish a paper on Ennius's *Annales,* and Benjamin seems pleased with it. He thinks you have a decent chance of publishing it. You have some ideas that should turn into good papers in the spring, if you work hard. You enjoy hard work.

It's not like you've turned into a monk. You avoid dating in the department—that's caused you enough trouble already. But you go to clubs, you pick up women. You've gotten good at picking up women. The women in New York are pretty damn hot and easy to get out of those tiny dresses. You take them home, you get them naked, you have sex, everyone has a good time all around. Your cock buried in their cunts, their mouths, their asses. They seem to enjoy themselves. You fuck them hard, on the couch, on the bed, up against the wall. And then you don't call them. You don't call anyone, and no one calls you— you're thinking of getting your home phone disconnected.

Mostly, you don't even want to see the women again. And on the rare occasions when you do think, *Hmmm, it might be nice to see her again,* it doesn't take long before your common sense reasserts itself. Just a glimpse of Belinda's wounded eyes in the department, or a memory of all those terrible months post-Sarah, is enough to remind you that getting involved with women causes trouble. You meet them, you fuck them, and you get on with your successful academic life. It's not exactly what you expected when you moved to New York, but it's nothing to sneeze at, either. Maybe someday you'll meet a woman who will change your mind. But you're not looking for one.

THE END

It was a good blow job, no question. But seeing a man kneeling there, at your feet, with his mouth still wet with your come, makes your stomach do flip-flops. Now that the blow job is over, you can't help thinking about what it would be like to reciprocate—putting your mouth on some other guy's cock. Just the thought is making you feel light-headed. Maybe it would be more enlightened of you if you could do it, go down on a guy. Maybe it would mean that you were secure in your own masculinity. But you can't force yourself to be comfortable with it—and at least for now, you feel like you don't ever want to do anything like this again. Which means that what you say next is no fun. "Rick, that was great, really. . . ."

"But?" He looks up at you, from his kneeling position at your feet. He's got a puppy-dog expression on his face, like he's about to be kicked. Ouch.

"I don't think I can do this kind of thing." You shrug apologetically. You're not sure what else to say.

"Hey, no biggie." Rick stands up quickly, shakes your hand. He squeezes hard enough to hurt. "Enjoy the rest of the party." And then he's turning and walking away. Rhonda gives you a quick kiss on your cheek. "Too bad, sweetie. Could've been lots of fun." And then she joins her husband, walking across the room, disappearing into the kitchen.

You feel like you've just had a very narrow escape, though you're not sure from what or whom. You go in search of Wendy—maybe she can help you sort all this out.

When you find Wendy, she's not in any condition to talk to you. She's up against a curving marble pillar, being fucked by a massive black man. He's at least twice as wide as she is, with broad shoulders and a thick torso; his skin is sheened with sweat, and he's slamming into her, hard. He's fucking in a pounding rhythm: rearing back and thrusting forward, jack-knifing in and up, digging deeper and deeper with each thrust as if he's trying to drill his cock up into Wendy's womb. He's gripping her waist in a bear hug, and each time he rears back, his butt squats outward before launching upward, lifting her feet off the ground.

It looks like it ought to hurt, like it should be tearing her apart, but Wendy seems to be enjoying herself, gasping with each thrust. Her head is tilted sideways, and her lips keep curving into a strange, distant smile. You feel like you ought to be upset watching this, but it really doesn't bother you. You're not sure why. A few people are standing around and watching; you could wait here. Or you could go chase down that Indian girl: she's standing near the door leading to the deck patio, watching the crowd, idly fingering her pussy. If you do that, you might miss your chance with Wendy.

- *If you want to wait for Wendy,* PLEASE TURN TO PAGE 174.

- *If you want to talk to the Indian girl,* PLEASE TURN TO PAGE 25.

It's almost irresistible, the temptation to go with it, sink your cock into her. But that's what she wants—she's trying to distract you with sex. You doubt Wendy is really as aroused as she seems, and it's a bit insulting that she's trying to manipulate you this way, that she even thinks it might succeed.

"Hey, enough of that." You pin her legs with yours, holding her steady beneath you, trying to ignore the promptings of your eager cock. "What's going on, Wendy?" You bend your head, gently rest your forehead against hers. "Talk to me."

Wendy's quiet, her eyes closed. She has stopped fighting you, stopped trying to seduce you; she's just lying underneath you. Long moments pass like that, until finally she says something so softly that you can't understand her.

"What?"

"I said, maybe we can bend just one rule." She opens her eyes and smiles up at you. Her face looks peaceful, relaxed. Something in your chest relaxes, too. You squeeze her briefly and then roll off her, still keeping an arm around her, keeping her close to you.

"I don't like this whole rule concept, Wendy. I don't even know what the other rules are."

She chuckles. "Maybe there aren't any other rules. Or maybe you won't know about them until you run into them." Wendy lifts up on one arm, drops a soft kiss against your lips. She doesn't usually kiss you. You like it. "Be content, Mark. You're the first guy I've let spend the night since I left my husband."

"Your what?" You'd been feeling smug at winning a victory, getting her to change one of her rules for you. You were sure it meant she cared about you, at least a little. But now you feel blindsided, like a massive truck came out of nowhere and slammed into you. Wendy's been married? You had no idea. The last remnants of your erection have disappeared.

"My husband. I'm married, Mark."

Not just *was* married, *is* married. You don't know what to say to that.

You don't say anything.

After a moment, Wendy continues, "We're separated—have been for years. Almost a decade, actually." She hesitates in the darkness of the bedroom, then rests her head against your chest and goes on. "I was still in college, a senior majoring in classics, when I met him; he was my favorite professor." You hold her close, content to listen to the story. You'll figure out how you feel about it when she's finished.

"I fell madly, hopelessly in love. Chased him until he gave in, had sex with me. He almost got fired over that, but by the time people found out, we were engaged. My parents had both died a year previously; car accident. So there wasn't really anyone to complain, and the trust made him sign some prenups before the wedding. Smart of them—I would have given him everything.

"We had three blissful years, and then one day I went to see him at the office and found him fucking one of his advisees. To make it worse, I was about to take my qualifying exams. His timing was rotten. I got so angry at Rufus that I threw him out. Chucked his stuff out the window. He had to move into a hotel for a while until he could find a place. He was so pathetic—he called, he wrote, he stood outside my window all night, waiting for me to look out and see him. I ignored him for weeks while I buried my head in my books and studied. Nursed my broken heart, aced the exams, and somehow, somewhere, in there, I lost the desire to ever take him back."

She shrugs, then pulls away to look up at you. "So, that's the sad story."

"**B**ut you're still married?" That seems to be the salient point, and one that hasn't been explained.

"Oh, well. It was easier. My lawyers send him a monthly check now. We see each other at parties." Wendy smiles. "It's all very civil."

"I see." You don't, really. Does it mean she still wants to be with this Rufus guy? Is that why she never got a divorce? Is she still in love with him?

"Hey." She kisses you again—twice in one night. That might be a record. It's a gentle kiss, a soft brush against your lips. "I'm perfectly willing to divorce Rufus. Just never had a good reason to."

"I see." And there's something relaxing in your belly. You've been dating her only a few months, and you don't know what you want from the future. But it's nice to know that there are possibilities. That's all you wanted to know.

You roll her over, pinning her underneath you again. You bend down and kiss her, your lips warm against hers, your tongue darting out to press against her teeth, and then, as her mouth opens under yours, to dance with her tongue, tangling. You kiss her for a long time, your hands coming up to cup her face. You kiss her forehead, her closed eyelids, her cheeks, her nose and chin. Eventually, the kissing turns to something more; eventually, she's breathing heavy, shifting underneath you, her body curving up to meet yours, her thighs opening for you.

And you're sliding in, burying your cock inside her, your face against her scented hair. You're moving in and out as Wendy twists and arches and moans beneath you as she laces her fingers into your hair and pulls you down for another kiss, and another, and another. Your balls tighten and the come rises through you until you're coming, coming hard inside her. Afterward, as you drift off to sleep, knowing that for the first time you won't have to leave this bed before morning, you feel a tentative peace settle inside you.

In the morning, everything's different. You wake to the smell of bacon and eggs; Wendy isn't in bed, but when you wander naked out of the bedroom, across the large living room and long dining room, she's standing in the kitchen, wearing a simple white silk robe, pouring two cups of coffee. Orange juice is waiting, already poured.

"Morning." You reach out and pull her into an embrace, nuzzle her neck. Your cock is already hard; standard morning hard-on.

She rests against you for a second, then pulls back—not out of your arms entirely, just enough to look up at you. "I have no idea what you take in your coffee."

You chuckle. "A little milk. You?"

"Black." She smiles and picks up her cup, takes a sip. Then she pours some milk into yours.

"That doesn't surprise me." Of course Wendy Lake takes her coffee black. She couldn't have it any other way.

Wendy starts piling the plates onto a large tray. "I hope you don't mind if we take this back to bed. I only have one chair for the dining table. I'll have to get another one."

You're on the verge of protesting that she doesn't need to buy furniture for you, but you bite it back. If she wants to buy a chair so you can eat together, why should you complain? Simply because it's likely to cost a lot of money? She makes a great deal more money than you do—she probably always will. You're going to have to get used to that. Now that Wendy has started opening up, you're not about to let some stupid macho impulse get in the way of this relationship. "That sounds good."

"Great." She hands you the breakfast tray, with everything precariously balanced on it. You start walking back to the bed carefully. Wendy follows you, sipping her cup of coffee. "Hey, Mark—do you want to go to Greece on Thursday?"

You almost spill the tray. You catch yourself and walk it over to the bed and set it down. Then you turn to Wendy. "What did you say?"

She's looking at you over the rim of her coffee cup, a little hesitantly. "There's this conference in Athens on Greek philosophy and culture. But they've invited me to come speak, to give a small slide presentation on love and sex in ancient Greece. I'm sure it's meant to be more of a break for the presenters than anything else, but they're paying my way: airplane tickets, hotel, the works. If you'd like to come, I'd be happy to buy you a ticket."

"But for this Thursday? To buy international tickets so close to the date, it'll be outrageous."

"I've got plenty of miles; it won't be a problem. Don't worry about the money, Mark. The only question is whether you want to come."

It's not really a question, is it? It's starting to get cold here in New York. Early October, and already there's a chill in the air. Greece— bright sun, blue ocean, warm, sandy beaches. Not to mention all that history. You've never been to Greece. "I would love to come."

"Good," Wendy says, looking relieved. She puts down her coffee cup. "Now, eat. We don't have anything on campus until after lunch today, right? I want you full of energy for the rest of the morning."

You smile and sit down on the bed, scooping up a forkful of fluffy eggs. Tasty; apparently Wendy isn't a bad cook. Not that you can concentrate on the food—you're going to Greece!

• PLEASE TURN TO PAGE 120.

You're standing amid a swirl of people. They're sharply dressed, for the most part, more so than professors would have been in Chicago. They're excited, animated—it's the first department party after a summer away, the first chance most of them have to meet the new hires, the fresh meat. Some vapid blonde in a too-tight black minidress is chattering at you; she's so pleased to have another historiographer in the department. She puts a hand on your arm, eagerly, almost spilling your drink. Her breasts are bursting out of her dress. She wants to show you her current work. You're sure she wants to show you more than that. Departments are notorious for collegial flings. It's inevitable—all those undergrads, all those grad students, with their beautiful young bodies, coming in waves every single semester. Students are off-limits, more or less, but new faculty are fair game, especially if they're unattached. You're very unattached. You nod politely at her, but you can't manage an actual smile. You haven't smiled properly in months.

"Cally, you simply must share Mark. You've had him for half an hour now." It's Professor Benjamin, the man who hired you. Portly, avuncular, gay, he has a long-term partner with whom he seems quite content. He hasn't flirted with you once during the hiring process, for which you are profoundly grateful. You weren't so lucky with some of the other schools. Years of tae kwon do plus a summer of intensive gym time apparently have given you the type of body that gay men dream of. More than a few women like it, too, judging by the number of female professors flirting with you tonight. Not that it does you any good. There was only one woman you wanted, and you couldn't keep her.

You don't want her anymore, anyway. Or so you're desperate to believe.

Cally pouts and flounces away, more like a teenage cheerleader than a tenure-track professor with two decent books to her name. You've read her work and admire it. Too bad she's such a flake.

"How are you settling in, Mark? Met everyone?"

"I think so, yes. Everyone except her . . ." You lift your glass in the direction of the fireplace, where a tall, slender woman is holding court, surrounded by other academics. She's dressed splendidly, in an ice-blue dress that hugs the gentle curves of her body; her waist-length black hair falls straight and silky against it. For a brief moment, you imagine burying your face in that fall of hair. You wonder what she smells like, and your cock stirs in your pants.

"Ah, yes. Our famous Professor Wendy Lake." Benjamin frowns slightly. "You'll have to meet her at some point, but be careful, lad. She can be distracting, especially to young professors."

"I can imagine that." Your eyes are still fixed on her, noticing how her pale blue eyes seem to catch the light, almost as if they're actually made of ice. She turns and looks straight at you. Her gaze grows intent, almost predatory. You can't seem to turn away. Benjamin wasn't kidding. She is quite distracting.

Benjamin harrumphs, pulling your attention back to him. His frown has deepened, and his glance slides back and forth between you and Wendy Lake. "Are you familiar with the work of Adrienne Michaels? Tom Stewart? They're both in your field . . . or they were."

You try to think back; you haven't really been working this summer. "I think I've read some articles by Michaels—nothing recently, though."

"No, there hasn't been anything recently. But they were both doing good, solid work, quite promising . . . until they got involved with Lake."

"Involved?" What does he mean? Academically involved? Or in some other way?

"Just watch yourself. Lake's material is popular—she certainly gets a lot of attention with all her radio and TV appearances. Her books sell very well. But her work isn't . . ." He hesitates, as if searching for the right word. "Well, it isn't *rigorous*. You're at a delicate stage in your career, you want to be taken seriously, don't you?"

"Of course." You're finding it hard to take Benjamin's veiled hints seriously. You're sure you could handle yourself if you got *involved* with Wendy Lake. Your eyes slide back to her. She's laughing now, her head tilted back and her throat exposed. She looks wholly approachable, very feminine.

You glance back briefly at Benjamin's concerned face—he looks worried, paternal. It's irritating. You can't resist the urge to poke at him a little. "Professor, why do you dislike her so much? Is she too much of a woman for your department?"

She looks like quite a woman. What would she be like in bed? If she were naked, those long limbs spread beneath you, would she be responding to your touch, her breath coming faster, her eyes widening—or would she be laughing, like she is now? A small corner of your mind wonders if she is laughing at you, but you squish that thought immediately. That's Sarah talking, not you.

"Nonsense, boy! I have nothing against women." He's practically spluttering. "Why, some of our best faculty are women! Belinda Lundstrom is doing very fine work, for example."

You turn back to Benjamin. Wendy Lake is eye candy: nice to fantasize about, but you have no desire to approach her. "Just joking, Professor. You don't need to worry about me, honestly. I'm not likely to get into that sort of trouble." Not anymore. Not since Sarah.

"You say that now. Let's see what you say in a few months."

Before you can respond to that, another colleague comes up and pulls Benjamin away for an urgent discussion of this semester's course schedule. He gets in a final warning frown before he goes, and you tilt your glass at him in acknowledgment. Then you down it—you aren't usually much of a drinker, but getting through this party is taking some effort.

You're not used to socializing anymore; you've been alone for months. All summer it was you and the TV and the gym. When you weren't zoned out in front of the TV, you were working out, pushing your body harder and harder. You're in the best physical shape of your life: you can do hundreds of fingertip push-ups, bench-press three hundred pounds—but it doesn't really matter, does it? It was just something to fill the time until you moved to New York, until you started this job.

You haven't been able to concentrate on your work at all. Every time you open a book, you're assaulted with memories of Sarah. Sarah bringing you a hot meal while you studied. Sarah leaving work at the magazine early, running your errands for you, so you could work harder, concentrate on finishing your thesis. Sarah with her mouth open, shouting, angry at how much you had to work, how late you'd come home from the department, how little you helped out at home. Sarah pulling away, turning cold in bed. Sarah with her legs in the air, being fucked on your couch by some stranger. The images make it hard to concentrate.

"Can I get you a refill?" The voice is low, cool. You turn and are confronted by Wendy Lake, just inches away. You take a sharp breath, and you know what she smells like: snow and evergreens, like a forest in Sweden, with a hint of vodka underneath.

"I'm okay, thanks." Another drink would dull your wits, and you feel like you'll need all of them to deal with this woman. You hold out your hand. "I'm Mark Matthews. New professor."

"I know, Mark. And I bet you know who I am, don't you?" She's playful, almost kittenish. It seems wrong on her, or if not wrong, then a bit disjointed. If she's a feline, she's not a kitten—she's a cheetah, a jaguar, playing briefly with her food before she tears it apart and swallows it down.

"Professor Lake. Of course. It's nice to meet you." You *can* stay in control of this conversation. You simply need to keep it friendly, professional.

"It's Wendy. Call me Wendy, Mark." Her voice is the tiniest bit seductive . . . you think. It could all be in your head. "Unless you want to call me something else." Okay, *that* tone wasn't in your head.

"Like what?" That wasn't the right response. That was asking for trouble. Maybe trouble is what you want.

"Surely you can think of something." The overtones are clearly there, the teasing, sexual challenge. The famous Wendy Lake is flirting with you. You're not going to back down from a challenge.

"I can think of a lot of things, Professor. But I'm not sure what would be appropriate." You're enjoying this—the flirting, the back-and-forth. It surprises you; it's been a long time since you've done this kind of thing, a long time since you've wanted to. Of course, it's been a long time since a woman as attractive as Wendy Lake has approached you. If one ever has.

She doesn't smile, but her eyes are locked on yours. *"Appropriate?"* she asks slowly, drawing out the syllables.

You hesitate, then go for it, curious as to how she'll respond. "Well then, Wendy Lake, Ph.D., what would you like me to call you?"

She leans in, and her voice drops to something intimate, seductive. "I'll let you know in my office. Room 309. Five minutes?"

Harmless flirting has suddenly turned to something very different.

Is this what you want? It seems clear what she's offering. Sex in a department office with one of your colleagues, one of the people with whom you'll be working, someone you've just met. You aren't in the habit of having sex with strangers; you don't know this woman at all.

On the other hand, you *thought* you knew Sarah. You thought you knew her intimately.

It's been a long time since you had sex.

• *If you agree to meet Wendy,* TURN TO PAGE 2.

• *If you don't agree to meet her* TURN TO PAGE 47.

"Hello, Mark."

"Wendy."

"I'm naked, Mark. I'm lying on my bed with my fingers in my cunt. I've been thinking about you. You have a hot body, Mark—and a sexy cock. It's nice and thick. I like your cock a great deal."

"You're killing me, Wendy. Let me come over."

"There's something about a sexy male body—all that strength, power. It shouldn't be covered up—it should be noticed, appreciated. I appreciate your body, Mark. And I want other people to notice your body, to think about it, to desire it. That turns me on, Mark—thinking about other people seeing you, wondering what you look like naked. Wondering if you have a hot body under your clothes. In our culture," she pauses, "there isn't enough appreciation for the nude male physique."

"Wendy?"

"Mark, do something for me." Her voice is low, teasing, seductive. "Take off your clothes, put on your shoes and coat, and come over. Don't take a cab. I want you to ride the subway, naked under your coat, thinking about fucking me."

"I could get thrown in jail, Wendy—someone's going to notice."

"I want people to notice, Mark. I want them to notice that you're not wearing pants—I want them to wonder if you're naked under that coat. Thinking about them watching you, wondering—that turns me on. It makes my pussy wet. Will you do that for me, Mark?"

• *If you do as she asks,* PLEASE TURN TO PAGE 42.

• *If this is going too far for you,* PLEASE TURN TO PAGE 193.

The pair of you dress quickly and head outside; Indira quickly flags a cab and gives an address somewhere on the Bowery. The taxi flies downtown, past Lincoln Center and the intriguing Flatiron Building on lower Fifth Avenue. Driving through New York at night is still a thrill for you. So much life! You are exhilarated, and in that moment you understand all the fuss over this city. It's funny, but you realize that you feel at home for the first time in your life.

Indira is sitting on your lap, looking out the cab window with you. You love it that she is grooving out on Manhattan with you, not insisting that you have some conversation. She smells sweet, like jasmine. The cab pulls up at an old municipal building. It's a renovated apartment building, Indira tells you. Every floor is a loft. When you finally walk inside, the space seem cavernous and the party endless, throbbing with techno music. Girls in skimpy tops dance, grinding their hips against boys in tight jeans.

Indira disappears into the crowd, promising to return. She leaves you contemplating the dancers. They're only a few years younger than you, but you feel decades older. You've never been much of a dancer anyway, and the sound filling the space, pulsing, doesn't have any recognizable tune. But then Indira's back, sliding her arms around you, fitting her hips to yours, and you might not know dancing, but you know sex, and that's what this is. Half the couples on the floor aren't dancing anyway; they're making out, hands pulling up shirts to bare small young breasts, hands unbuttoning jeans, sliding inside. It's all mostly covered, but it's happening, and in the darker corners, there is actual screwing going on, girls with their legs wrapped around the guys, fucking against the walls.

You can do this. You slide your hands over Indira's clingy top, a brightly painted image of Ganesha moving under your fingers with the motion of her heavy breasts. You pinch her nipples through the fabric, bend down, and suck on her ear, her neck. She moans and then turns her head for a kiss. You kiss her and feel a small round tablet slipping from her mouth to yours. You swallow it—it's what you came for, isn't it? You feel a brief moment of apprehension, wondering what it is. Indira notices and whispers reassuringly, "It's only X." Then she's kissing you again, her full lips moving against yours, her tongue darting out and touching your teeth, the top of your mouth. It's not long before you're pushing her through the crowd to a dark corner, not long until she's sliding down to her knees, unzipping your pants, and taking your cock in her agile mouth. Not long before you start feeling like everything's right with the world, everything's absolutely wonderful.

After you come, you rest against the wall with Indira's head in your lap, watching the crowd. You really like this girl. It's not like with Wendy. No mind games, no tests. And even with Sarah, whom you loved, you never felt this relaxed and content. Indira's something special, and you realize that you don't want anything more than to stay here with her in this blissful moment. You tell her this—you tell her how happy you are, being here with her. She smiles and cuddles into your arms; she doesn't say much, but she seems happy, too. You realize that you've been making a huge mistake, worrying so much about your job, about academia, even about Wendy. All you needed to do was take a step back, relax. Everything makes sense when you think about it the right way. You understand now how wonderful life can be when you're in the right place with the right person. You're not just happy—you're euphoric, utterly at peace with the world. Finally, you've learned how to live.

The bliss lasts a long time. Hours. You spent much of that time touching Indira, enjoying the softness of her skin, the scent of her hair. You slowly make her come, with your fingers moving idly in her pussy and her skirt hiked up to her hips; you watch her coming and think that you've never seen anything so beautiful in your life. Wendy Lake is a distant memory, and Sarah is practically forgotten. It's all about Indira—her dark eyes, her slightly tilted nose. When she finally gets up to use the bathroom, you don't want to let her go. But she promises to come back soon.

You start to feel the world returning, with all its frustration, its stress and upset. Your stomach churns, and suddenly you're shaking. You pull your knees up to your chin, wrap your arms around your legs, close your eyes. You can feel the bliss disappearing, the euphoria fading. It makes you want to cry. That's when someone taps on your shoulder.

"Hey, you look like you could use another one of these. Thirty bucks."

A boy is holding out a pink pill with a heart carved on it. You dig into your pants pocket, pull out your wallet. You're reaching for the money when you suddenly wonder if this is such a good idea.

• *If you buy the pill*, PLEASE TURN TO PAGE 131.

• *If you don't buy it*, PLEASE TURN TO PAGE 44.

In the next few weeks, you throw yourself into your teaching. You spend long days working up lesson plans, reviewing student papers, meeting in office hours. Your students start to like you; they linger after class to talk about classics. Benjamin says if you keep it up, you might win a teaching award next year. You feel a quiet satisfaction as the Christmas break starts; you're making something of yourself at last. Now you need to get some research done, publish a few papers.

It's snowing outside on the afternoon you meet the girl. You're wandering aimlessly through the library, thinking about an issue in *Lysistrata* that might merit a small article. The library's almost deserted—only the most industrious students are here working over the holiday. You're in the depths of the stacks, so distracted that you turn a corner and walk right into a young woman standing and highlighting furiously in a small library book, Foucault's *History of Sexuality,* volume 2. You remember reading that in grad school; it was one of your favorite books. You can't believe she's writing in a library book. "Hey, what are you doing?"

She frowns up at you. "Why do you care?" She's a slender woman, part Asian, it looks like. Her black hair is cut short, spiked with streaks of dark purple and bright blue. She's quite pretty.

You try to sound older, stern. "Young lady, I'm on the faculty here."

Her eyes widen, and she suddenly looks worried. "What field?"

"Classics. What difference does that—"

"Oh, good." She relaxes. "Want a blow job?"

• PLEASE TURN TO PAGE 234.

Y ou want her badly—badly enough to do this, even though your gut is churning at the thought. And, to be honest, despite the disgust, there's also a rush of arousal moving through you as you lean on one elbow, your eyes locked on hers. There's a thrill, giving over your will to her like this, watching her watch you, leaning forward, and taking the finger in your mouth. It tastes . . . salty. Normal. Like a finger normally tastes. You bathe it with your tongue, confused. Then you pull back, letting it pop out.

She grins at you. "Were you expecting something else? Wrong hand for that, sweetheart."

Just another of her petty games. You feel a wave of frustration mixed with relief. And a secret pleasure; you've pleased her, and she's happy with you. You're eager to see what your reward will be. "So, what now?"

"Now? Now you go home, Mark." She slides off the bed, walks to the hallway. You don't have much choice but to follow. You pull on your clothes, slowly. You don't want to leave her. Every moment you spend with Wendy Lake, you feel more intense, more alive. "That's it?"

Wendy shrugs. "This was fun, but I've had enough for tonight. Did you want something more?"

"Yes." You walk toward her, pull her into your arms. She doesn't resist, exactly, but she doesn't melt in to you, either. She tilts her head up, looks inquisitively at you.

"How much more?"

You smile, tentatively. "Lots more?" You want to fuck her again, fuck her up against one of those rough brick walls.

She pulls out of your arms then, steps away, crossing her arms across her naked breasts. It's not an inviting pose. "What are you doing tomorrow?"

You want to throw her onto the bed and screw her brains out, but apparently that's not going to happen. She wants to play more games instead. If that's what she wants, "There's the Matthews seminar—"

Wendy nods. "Meet me at the Cloisters instead. At two. And remember—no underwear."

"I haven't forgotten." You shouldn't be skipping academic responsibilities this soon, but Wendy wants you to. And you had been meaning to visit the Cloisters; the medieval tapestries and monk's garden are legitimately related to your research. If anyone asks, you can say you were working.

"Good." She's walking down the hall, opening the front door, ushering you out. "Good night, Mark."

• PLEASE TURN TO PAGE 14.

"I don't think that's really my thing, Indira. Sorry."

"Oh, well—could've been fun. Anyway, thanks for the fucking. It was good." And then she's pulling away, standing up, and walking off.

Well. That was abrupt.

You get up, disconcerted, and walk back over to where it looks like Wendy and the big man are finally finishing up.

• PLEASE TURN TO PAGE 174.

"Tell me what you want, Wendy. You're a very sexy woman, and I'll probably let you do whatever you want, but I need to know what it is first."

Wendy says, "I want to suck your cock." She says it matter-of-factly, in the same tone you might tell your students, "I want you to read thirty pages of Saint Augustine tonight." With the same expectation of compliance.

"Is that really a good idea?" As good as a blow job sounds, you can't help being aware that there are people right outside. At any moment, someone could knock on the door, stick their head in to ask a quick question. And besides, this is all going pretty damn fast. Fucking last night, blow job today—what's happening with this woman? "Shouldn't we talk about all this?"

Wendy frowns and leans back against the window. "I'm not really that interested in talking to you, Mark. I'm in to fucking." She licks her lips, the tip of her tongue traveling in a slow circle, starting your balls throbbing. "I thought you were, too. If you're not, leave. The door is right behind you." Then she grins—it's not a nice grin. It's nasty. "And you don't have to worry—I won't tell anyone that all you wanted to do with me was talk." Wendy blows you a sarcastic kiss.

"I just want to be clear on what's happening here." You know you're risking annoying her, but this is developing into a tricky situation. It makes you nervous, not having any idea what's going on in this woman's head. Benjamin did warn you about her.

"What's happening is sex, Mark. What did you think was happening?" She's mocking you.

"Sex is fine, Wendy, but . . ." You hesitate.

"Dear boy." Wendy laughs softly. "Don't tell me that you're still looking for true love? After that fiasco with your girlfriend?"

"You know about that?" How would she know about Sarah?

"Everyone knows, Mark. People here know people at the U of C. How could we not know? Really, everyone in the department knows about the poor, brokenhearted young professor. If you're looking for *comforting,* well, there are plenty of other ladies and gentlemen in our department who'd love to help you with that."

Fine. Everyone knows about you and Sarah. They probably even know why you broke up, how you came home and found her . . . You can worry about that later. "I didn't say I wanted comforting."

"So, what do you want?" She sounds impatient.

You don't want to get screwed. Not figuratively, at any rate. "I want to know what you want. You've got something of a reputation yourself, Professor Lake. I want to know what I'm letting myself in for."

"Well, I wanted to give you a blow job. However, I seem to have lost all interest in that idea."

"Fine, then." If that's the way she wants to be, she can go screw herself. You nod curtly, then turn to open the door. Before you can, she says, "Okay, okay. Don't be such a juvenile. Why don't you call me tonight?" She scribbles a number on a Post-it with a Montblanc pen. "I might be in a different mood then."

You smile slowly. She can't see your face. You've won a small victory—you think. "I'll do that."

• PLEASE TURN TO PAGE 152.

"I don't want to give up on us, Wendy. Can't you meet me halfway, at least?" You step farther into the room, your hands outstretched, pleading.

Her arms are crossed tight over her chest, shielding her breasts. "I can't promise you any happy-ever-afters, Mark. I've been married before—I have no desire to be married again."

You could scream with frustration or bang your head against the wall. "Did I say *anything* about marriage? All I'm asking is that we be a normal couple for a while—a normal, sexually exclusive couple." You cross the room, take Wendy's hands in yours, pulling them down from their defensive position.

Wendy looks troubled, but she doesn't take her hands away. "Forever? Never have sex with anybody else ever again?"

"Is that so important to you?" You've never met a woman like her. Isn't it supposed to be the guy complaining about never getting to have sex with other women?

Wendy shrugs slightly, frowning. "I don't know. Maybe it is. I haven't been monogamous in a very long time, Mark. I'm not sure I believe in it."

You can understand that much, at least. When you came home and found Sarah with that guy, you thought you'd never trust anyone again. And now, with Wendy, you came very close to walking out that door. But you cared about this woman too much to walk out without even trying. You squeeze her hands, trying to think of a solution. But then you realize maybe you don't need a solution right away, or not a complete one, anyway.

"Wendy, look. We can figure that out later, can't we? Whether it's what we want for forever? Can we compromise for now? Say, monogamy for six months, see how it goes? If we like it, great, if not, we'll renegotiate then."

She's still frowning, but it's shifted. It's not a hopeless frown—more of a meditative one. "One month."

She's got to be kidding! "One month is hardly anything! Three months."

Wendy grins suddenly and lets go of your hands, but only to step into your arms. "Done." She wraps her arms around you and squeezes hard. "And I'm sorry about Stavros," she adds quietly.

"I'll get you for that later, don't worry. You'll be sorry." You're still angry on some level, but it's barely noticeable under the tidal wave of relief sweeping through you. Relief and something else, something that feels oddly like hope.

• PLEASE TURN TO PAGE 108.

Y ou can't resist her when she's like this. You slide into her pussy, and it feels so good. She rolls you over and rides you, her hair hanging down to hide her face, her body rising and falling above you. Her breasts hang down in this position, looking larger than they are, the nipples dark and firmly erect. Your hands come up to grip her hips, guiding her motion; her fingers dig in to your chest, each one a tiny point of pain that blurs into the rest of the sensation, heightening it, and all the while she's still whispering to you, or to herself, "Yes, yes, fuck, yes, oh, God, like that, yes," whispering and whimpering and moving faster and faster until she's coming, coming hard, her mouth opening in a scream, her head thrown back.

This is where you usually move faster, where you come, too, but instead, she's keeping control, she's moving again, her thighs pressing against yours, slowing you down. She's sliding down, resting against your chest, but her hips are still moving, still fucking, faster, then slower, then faster again, but never quite fast enough for you to come. She knows you well enough to know exactly how to do that. It goes on and on and on, until it's almost dawn, and you're shaking with tiredness. Only then, then, does she finally relax, finally let you take over, and you're almost too tired, but you manage to move faster, fast enough, until you come, explosively, for endless minutes. You've never come so hard, for so long. That may have been the best sex you've ever had.

Afterward, you can't move, you can't think. You fall asleep.

Y ou wake feeling a quiet triumph—the sunlight is slanting onto the bed through the shutters, and it's the first time you've woken in her apartment, the first time she's let you stay the night. Though, technically, it wasn't night when you fell asleep. Wendy isn't in bed, but you can smell food—bacon, eggs. You get up, walk out to the kitchen. She isn't there, either, but there's a plate of breakfast food waiting for you, along with juice and milk and coffee. When you pick up the plate, you find a note underneath it, written on a plain white sheet of paper.

Mark, you want more of me than I can give. I'm sorry, but it's over. I hope you enjoyed last night. Please don't call me again.

And that's it. She isn't anywhere in the apartment. You're bewildered—you go back to the bedroom, sit down on the bed, try to think back over the events of the night before. Everything was going so well. You had sex, it was good. Then you asked her to let you stay the night. She warned you not to push. You pushed anyway—and then she freaked out, with the hitting and the shouting. It had startled you, but you'd thought it was a good thing, that it meant you were getting through to her. And the sex afterward was intense, raw, passionate. It was exactly what you wanted, wasn't it?

Of course it wasn't. You're an idiot. What you *wanted* was to get Wendy to talk to you, to open up. That was the goal. When you started breaking through to her, you should have kept her talking, taken that tiny window of emotion and pried it wide open. Instead, you took the sex she offered—the distraction that let her avoid talking to you. You've made a huge mistake, but it can't be over, can it? Wendy's got to give you another chance.

You leave breakfast untouched; you go home, planning how you'll talk her around. You leave Wendy messages on her voicemail, asking to see her again, asking what you've done wrong, promising to make it right, if she'll give you another chance. But she doesn't answer your calls.

You never seem to catch her alone in the department—she's always talking to a student or a colleague, and when you try to catch her eye for a moment alone, she looks right past you. Even hanging around outside her apartment door doesn't work—you don't know how she does it, but you never even see her there. For weeks, months, you don't talk to Wendy Lake at all.

What can you do? There's only so long a grown man can chase a grown woman. In January, after the Christmas holidays, you start dating again. You don't want to spend another Christmas alone.

You meet a nice woman in the German department, Anja. You meet for coffee; you visit the Met. On your third date, you take her to dinner at Sylvia's to share messy ribs and collard greens. Anja has never had soul food before, but by the time the sweet potato pie comes around, she's declaring herself a devoted fan. You're splitting your slice of pie—Anja has finished her own—when you see Wendy Lake. She's across the restaurant, eating fried chicken with two other women—one East Asian, one all-American redhead. It's been long enough that you're noticing other women again, and both of them are quite attractive. Still, it's Wendy that your eyes focus on—her clean profile, her mobile lips. She's laughing with her friends, talking, licking her fingers clean. She glances at you, once—she knows you're there. But when you would have gotten up, would have gone to speak with her, to say something, she shakes her head, just a little, with those pale blue eyes locked on yours. She looks wistful but resolved.

What can you do? You give her what she wants, with a small nod of your head. You say good-bye, silently. Whatever your future holds, it won't hold any more of Wendy Lake.

You turn back to Anja and try to enjoy your date.

THE END

It's a long haul to Rick and Rhonda's Long Island home, over an hour on the LIRR. You don't mind the hike, though—it gives you time to process everything that's been happening to you . . . and time to get excited, aroused, thinking about Rhonda again, and Rick, and their mysterious friend. Rick offered to pick you up at the station, but since they live only a few blocks away, you said you'd rather walk. You arrive at their doorstep a few minutes after eight. You ditched a department party for this; you can't bring yourself to care that Professor Benjamin will be wondering where you are. Maybe Wendy Lake will be wondering, too. If so, it'll do her good to miss you.

Rhonda greets you at the door, all smiling housewife in a simple blue dress and white apron. You realize you don't know if she has a job; you don't know what either of these people do—in fact, you don't know anything about them at all, except that they're fun to fuck. They could be serial killers who make a practice of picking up people at sex parties and luring them to their home. But before you can get too worried about it, Rhonda's closing the door and stepping in for a wet, sloppy kiss, sliding one hand down to grab your dick and fondle it.

"Hey, lover. Come meet Kimmie."

You follow her, already aroused, into a lovely old-fashioned house. Every inch of wall space is covered with framed art photographs, watercolors, antique mirrors, and oversize World War I posters. The kitchen is wide open and sun-filled. It all seems so genteel and comfortably middle-class. A slender redhead is sitting on a couch against the kitchen's far wall. She looks thoroughly respectable, too, in a white tank top and blue jeans. Rick is dressed in jeans and a T-shirt; you can smell the grill going in back. Burgers. Hamburger buns, a bowl of potato salad, and ketchup are on the wide marble kitchen counter. For a moment, despite Rhonda's kiss, you wonder if you misunderstood—maybe this really is just dinner.

"Mark, this is Kimmie."

"Hey, Mark." And then Kimmie is off the couch, walking over to you. She has to stand up on her tiptoes to kiss you. But she seems perfectly willing to do that; her mouth opens as soon as it touches yours, and before you can think twice, your tongues are entangled, and you're sliding your hands down to cup her hips and pull her closer to you. Then you're being pulled into the deepest, wettest kiss you've ever had. When you finally come up for air, Kimmie is grinning up at you.

"So, will he do, Kimmie?" Rhonda asks.

"He'll do just fine. The only question is, does he want dinner now or later?"

"Dinner later is fine with me." The burgers smell great, but they can wait. All you want to do is peel Kimmie out of those tight jeans. You hadn't expected things to go quite this fast, but you aren't about to complain.

Rick grins. "Then just follow me. Rhonda, honey, can you get the burgers?"

She nods. "No problem. I'll be up in a minute."

You follow Kimmie up the stairs, with Rick trailing behind you. She walks through an open door into what is clearly the master bedroom. Delicate roses cover the wallpaper, and a massive bed, dressed with soft-looking lavender sheets, takes up most of the room. Not exactly how you had pictured a sex den. But what surprises you more than the furnishings are the other items in the room—cameras. Video cameras. One in each corner, plus a fancier one on a wheeling dolly.

Kimmie asks, "Do you mind if Rick tapes us? It really turns me on." And she's kissing you again, unbuttoning your shirt and pulling it off so eagerly that it's hard for you to think about anything else. You've never been taped before, but the idea of watching the tape later, watching your bodies together, your cock in her cunt on-screen, is exciting. You wonder if you'll look good on tape. You want to know.

"Fine with me." You're pulling off her tank top, exposing smallish breasts, very pale and lightly freckled. You're licking her neck, pushing her back toward the bed. She's falling willingly onto it, and you're kissing her breasts, taking the thick pink nipples in your mouth, sucking them gently at first, then harder, while your hands unbutton and unzip her jeans. Then you're kissing down her stomach, kneeling on the floor at the foot of the bed, peeling the jeans off. Kimmie's not wearing panties, and her bush is dark red and curly. You can't resist the urge to tug a curl gently—it springs back into place when you let go. Then you're diving down, taking her cunt in your mouth, and it's sweet. You lick and nibble, and she's making all the right noises, whimpering and arching.

That's when Rick says, "Could you guys scootch to the right?" You glance up, and the camera's right there, a few feet away, Rhonda standing right next to it, watching you, the tip of her tongue visible between her slightly parted lips.

This is weird, but you're not about to stop now. You move to the right as asked, and Rick smiles and gives you a thumbs-up. Then you go back to what you're doing, oddly conscious of the camera fixed on your mouth, on Kimmie's wet pussy. It turns you on, being watched like this. You glance back to see Rick unzipping his pants, pulling out his dick and stroking it while he tapes you. Rick's enjoying himself, it seems, and Rhonda must be too, 'cause she's crouching down next to you on the carpet, taking off your shoes and socks, undoing your belt, unzipping your pants. You lift up enough for her to ease them off, and then she's pulling off her dress, revealing that she's not wearing any underwear either. Is this how all Long Island housewives dress, ready to fuck and be fucked at a moment's notice?

Rhonda's urging you up onto the bed, so you climb up there, and Kimmie is sliding back, too, and then you go down again. You're surprised to feel the bed shifting as Rhonda climbs onto it behind you; she's slipping beneath you, her mouth eagerly swallowing your cock, and this feels great, this feels better than the sixty-nine you managed to get Sarah to do a few times. Maybe because nothing is distracting Rhonda—she's concentrating entirely on sucking you off, her mouth slurping against the base, the shaft, her tongue bathing every inch of your cock. Kimmie's whimpers are getting louder; she's arching and twisting on the bed, one hand buried in your hair, the other clenched in the bedsheets.

You're trying to do a good job, licking her clit in long, slow strokes, but it's hard to concentrate with Rhonda's mouth on your cock. You want to focus on Kimmie, on the slightly fruity scent of her, the shape of her pussy with its heavy lips and large clit, to be able to remember it later, to distinguish it from the other women you've had this week, but you can't focus, it's too much, it's overwhelming. Rhonda's mouth is moving faster on you, and you can't help it, you move faster, too, press harder against Kimmie's clit, licking and sucking, and it doesn't seem to matter that you aren't using any skill at all—she's coming anyway, coming hard against your mouth. Even with Rhonda's mouth busy on your cock, you notice that not once do Kimmie's legs come up around your head—not once does she make any move that'll block the camera's view.

It's strange, noticing that. It's disappointing that you couldn't make her lose control, but exciting that you'll be able to watch this later and see every inch, watch your mouth moving on her, watch her coming against you. The thought of that is exciting enough that you start pumping harder against Rhonda's mouth, your groin clenches, and you feel the jism rising up, spurting out. She's pulled out, you're not coming in her mouth, you're coming all over her face, long streaks of white, and her head is thrown back against the bed, and you hope the camera's catching it all.

Afterward, it's awkward. You're not sure what to say to them, to these strangers, really, whom you've just been fucking. Rick's eyes are still glued to the camera—he's fiddling with buttons— maybe replaying something. He says in an abstracted voice, "You guys looked great, just terrific."

You wonder what part he's watching. Kimmie moves down the bed, kisses you, and says, "Nice job!"

"Thanks," you say. You've never been in this sort of situation before. It's a relief when Rick hands the camera over to Rhonda, takes off his pants, and comes over to start sucking your balls. Now it's sex again—you can do sex. Sex is easy.

You take turns fooling around, fucking, operating the camera. When Kimmie's stomach starts rumbling, you break for dinner, burgers out back, accompanied by oddly clinical conversation about sex and camera angles. Rick is obsessed with the camera, with getting perfect shots—he goes on and on about foreshortening and ways to overcome that effect. You're not really participating in the conversation; you don't have any interest in videography. And it's not as if these people can discuss your academic work with you; they don't have the background. You're not here for the conversation, anyway. You bolt your burger and then wait impatiently for the rest of them to finish, so you can all go upstairs for more sex. You can't wait to see what'll happen next.

When you do get upstairs again, you don't end up doing anything more serious with Rick, but you do fuck his wife with him—you in her cunt and him in her ass, while Kimmie operates the camera. Your legs brush against his at times, and you're glad that it doesn't bother you—it feels great, shoving into Rhonda's cunt with Rick's thick cock pressing into her ass, making everything tight and hot. His cock presses against yours, separated only by a thin wall of muscle; it's almost as if you're rubbing cocks together, and the thought of that turns you on even more.

Afterward, you go down two flights to the furnished basement. A massive audio-video setup is there: a projection TV, speakers all around the room. Rick mixes martinis at the built-in bar; when they're ready, you settle down into a long, overstuffed black leather sofa—Kimmie, then you, then Rhonda, then Rick—and watch the tape. It looks surprisingly good; there are moments that aren't so flattering to you or the others, but you all have pretty attractive bodies and are reasonably athletic; it makes for hot sex that looks good on camera.

"So, what do you think, Mark?" Rick is pouring you another drink, smiling.

"It looks good," you say, taking the drink. "Could I get a copy?"

"Definitely. And you don't mind if we keep copies ourselves?" He's still standing in front of you, blocking your view of the tape. It's started running a second time; you can't take your eyes off it.

"No, that's fine." They seem like nice people—and if you can trust them enough to fuck them, surely you can trust them enough to leave a smutty videotape with them. Though you'd be in some trouble if that showed up anywhere. College professors aren't really supposed to do this kind of thing—or if they do, they're not supposed to get caught doing it.

"Great." Rick isn't moving, still standing in front of you, looking down at where you sit, holding your drink in one hand while the other lingers on his wife's shoulder. "Then I have one more question for you—what do you think about our selling this tape?"

For a moment, you can't quite breathe; your fingers inadvertently squeeze Rhonda's shoulder, and she makes a small sound. You release her, apologetically stroking her shoulder, before answering Rick. "You're joking."

"No, we're quite serious. This is how we make our living," Rick says quietly.

Your face must show some of the alarm you're feeling, because Rhonda immediately leans over and rests a reassuring hand on your arm. "We would *never* sell this without your permission. Your written permission. I promise."

"That's good to know." You feel better. You'd had visions of your students showing up to class, laughing at you because they'd watched you naked, fucking, on late-night cable the night before.

Rick goes on to explain in more detail. "Rhonda and I sell the tapes online; we usually pay the actors, our friends, anywhere from two hundred to five hundred dollars per scene. Kimmie's one of our regulars; she makes enough from these tapes to support herself and her daughter."

"You have a daughter?" You'd never have guessed—she looks so young, so innocent.

Kimmie nods. "And a deadbeat ex-husband. And a good plastic surgeon who did a great job getting rid of the stretch marks."

"There were several great scenes in that material—if you're up for it, we can pay you a thousand dollars for your share. The same to Kimmie, of course."

A thousand dollars, almost a month's rent—for a few hours of fucking. It's a good deal; a hell of a lot better than the measly $35K they pay for a year of work at the university. A lot more fun, too. But it's a risky proposition—if word gets out, it might ruin your academic career. On the other hand, Rick and Rhonda probably have a lot of attractive friends for you to fuck. And it's definitely flattering, to have them think they can sell videos of you having sex. You like the idea that other men will be watching these tapes, jerking off, wishing they could do what you're doing, fuck the women you're fucking. You could be an amateur porn star in your spare time. And it's not that likely anyone in the department will find out. Besides, who would have the nerve to say anything if they did?

"So, what do you say, Mark? Can we sell this tape?"

• *If you say yes,* PLEASE TURN TO PAGE 8.

• *If you say no,* PLEASE TURN TO PAGE 30.

You give Belinda's hands one more quick squeeze, then let go. Belinda's biting her lip, and her eyes look oddly wet, as if she's about to start crying right here in public. You're not sure what's going on with her, but you don't want to climb into the middle of someone else's emotional mess. You've got plenty of your own to deal with.

"I don't think that would be a good idea." You've turned down two women in one week. Briefly, you think there must be something wrong with you. But this feels like the right decision. "I'm not looking to rush into sex." You're about to suggest taking it slower, becoming friends first—it's not like you'd never be interested in sleeping with her. But before you can say anything, Belinda stands up, steps away from the table.

"Of course. I'm so sorry, Mark. I don't know what came over me. You were being so friendly, and it's been so long since Joseph and I . . . Look, let's pretend this never happened, okay? I've got to run. I'll see you around the department." And before you can even rise from your chair, she's grabbed her purse and disappeared, leaving you alone with two cups of cooling coffee and the check.

It doesn't look like you're going to get a second chance with Belinda Lundstrom, either. Women in this city are just strange.

THE END

Does she really expect you to lie here and take that? It makes you feel sick, thinking of some other man touching her skin, sinking his cock into her pussy. You get up, start pulling on your pants. You wish you had underwear; it would be comforting right now to be able to more fully cover yourself.

"Mark?" Her voice sounds hesitant, uncertain. It would be tempting to think that meant you had a chance of convincing her to do what you want, to give her body to you alone. But you know better. With Wendy, everything has to be on her terms, the way she wants it. If you pushed, she'd end things. Better to do it yourself.

You don't say anything until you're fully dressed—shirt, socks, shoes. You'll grab your coat on your way out. You stand there a moment, just looking at her. In the half-light, lying across that massive, silken bed, she's more than beautiful. She's stunning. You know you'll never be with a woman that gorgeous again.

"Good-bye, Wendy."

She doesn't say anything to that. Just looks at you until you turn and walk away.

THE END

Screw wisdom. You want to fuck. You can't think about anything else.

"Right here is fine with me." You keep stroking her pussy with one hand while you unbutton your pants with the other. It isn't long before you're pushing Wendy up against your desk, sliding your naked cock into her hungry cunt. She leans back, braces her hands against the desk, slides her legs up around your waist. You fuck her hard, one hand at her back, holding her in position, the other pressed firmly against her mouth. She's whimpering, and you don't want anyone to hear a sound. Your cock is sliding in and out of her wet cunt, and she's squeezing you, pulsing around you. This is something Sarah doesn't know how to do—you're sure Wendy has lots of tricks that Sarah can't, or won't, do. You plan to experience them all, and maybe you can teach some of them to Sarah, too. Wendy is shoving her hips up to meet yours, moving faster and faster, and then she's coming, biting your hand and coming hard, and you're close, you're going to come, too.

That's when the door opens, and Sarah walks in.

"Mark—"

She doesn't say anything else . . . you'll never know what she was about to say. Maybe she left work early because she wasn't feeling well; maybe she was going to surprise you with office sex; maybe she just missed you. You can't stop fucking, not now, when you're so close to coming yourself. You thrust a few more times, come hard inside Wendy Lake, and then pull out and turn around to explain, your cock still dripping come down your thigh.

The door is wide open, and Sarah is gone.

She doesn't really have any reason to complain—you caught her exactly like this. But you know that argument won't work, since you won't even get the chance to make it. You took a stupid risk, and now you've lost her, she's on her way home to pack and leave for Chicago. You know her well enough to know that. You've lost the woman you love.

Fucking Wendy Lake seems cold consolation.

THE END

Y ou come back from Greece to New York in late autumn, early winter. It should be a depressing time, but you can't be depressed—not with Wendy opening up to you. It's a slow process; she lets you excavate small nuggets of information, bit by bit. It's been a long time since she's really talked to anyone. You try to be patient, and when you can't be patient, you have sex instead. It's always a great distraction.

The day before Halloween, Wendy makes you dinner. She's gotten that second chair. You'd threatened to put it at the far end of her ridiculously long dining table, but she'd laughingly insisted that you sit next to her instead. Her chair remained at the head of the table, though. She's never cooked dinner for you before—you're not sure what to expect. Normally, she eats at very fancy restaurants, far beyond your means. You're expecting something similar—something with truffle oil, or lobsters, or foie gras. Instead, she brings out two plates piled high with meat loaf and mashed potatoes, then adds a big bottle of ketchup to the table.

"Ketchup?" you ask as you sit down at the table.

"It makes everything better," Wendy says solemnly.

"Well, then I feel very lucky. You must actually like me."

Wendy smiles. "Either that or I want something from you."

"Oh?" You wonder what she could possibly want.

She hesitates. "See, there's sort of this traditional party I throw here every Halloween."

Parties are okay—you like parties. It would be kind of fun, actually, hosting a party with her. "We could have a party here. Do I have to dress up? Is it a costume party?"

"Not exactly. Unless not wearing clothes counts as a costume. It's a sex party." She glances at you, then hurries on before you can speak. "I'm not saying I want to have sex with someone there. We can wander around, enjoy the show, maybe do stuff with each other, if you're comfortable with that. But people will be disappointed if I cancel the party."

It's your turn to hesitate. You're curious about that kind of party, and you don't think you'll mind being naked in front of a bunch of strangers, as long as they're naked, too. But there's a bigger issue here.

"If I want you to, will you cancel the party?"

"Yes." She doesn't even hesitate, and she smiles at you when she says it.

"Then I don't need you to cancel it. Let's do it." You smile at her and then load up a forkful of meat loaf and mashed potatoes. It's good. Everything's good.

It's definitely strange, walking around a roomful of naked people, some of whom are having sex. It's easier with Wendy at your side. She introduces you to people, and they're perfectly normal introductions. Most of them have perfectly normal jobs, too—some academics, lots of writers and artists, a few rich people who don't seem to work at all. Some of their jobs aren't so normal.

"Mark, this is Rick and his wife, Rhonda. They run an amateur porn business out of their home in Long Island."

"It's nice to meet you both."

"Oh, he's a cutie, Wendy," Rhonda gushes. She's a rather overdone blonde with large silicone breasts. You can't help admiring her long shapely legs, though. "Mark, if you ever want to be in the movies, you should give us a call."

"Umm . . . thanks. I'll keep that in mind."

"Oh, Mark, come here, I want you to meet an old friend of mine,

Christian Blake. He's a politician, but very nice despite that." Wendy has drifted a few steps away; she's talking to an immense black man, very tall and very broad, with a mass that's mostly muscle. You nod politely to Rick and Rhonda and turn to join Wendy. Christian is bending over her hand, turning it in his, and dropping a kiss on the wrist. Smooth.

"More than just a friend, I hope, dear Wendy. Might you be available later this evening? I would love to remind you of what you may have forgotten." He leers at her in a surprisingly charming, friendly way.

Christian has a heavy, thick cock—you can't help staring at it. You doubt Wendy could forget that, but before you can start to worry, she's laughing, taking her hand back from him. "Not tonight, dear. I'm saving myself for Mark."

The large man takes your hand in two of his and shakes it vigorously. "Well, I'm impressed. You must be something, young man. You'd better be good to our Wendy, you understand?"

"Yes, sir. I'll do my best." You can't help it—you want to dislike the man, knowing that he's had sex with Wendy, but you can't. There's something immensely open and likable about him. He must be a very good politician.

"Christian, we'll talk to you later, okay? I think Indira was hoping to spend some time with you." There's a young Indian woman standing a few steps behind Christian, looking very hopeful indeed. Christian says good-bye and goes to join the woman. It isn't long before they're kissing, her small brown body pressed up against his large black one— you almost want a set of charcoals to sketch them with.

Wendy watches them fondly. "Indira's a very promising young

artist; I have some of her work in a gallery I own, and it's selling like mad. And she's ravenous in bed. I think Christian will like her."

"I didn't know you owned a gallery, Wendy."

She grins. "There's a lot you don't know about me."

"That's very true." You bend down to kiss her. From the corner of your eye, you can see that Christian and Indira have already moved to fucking, using one of Wendy's large marble pillars for support. It's inspiring, and watching their hips moving together makes you want Wendy's hips against yours, her breasts pressed against your chest. She responds eagerly, her hands coming up to cup your face, her mouth moving under yours. Your cock grows hard, and as you gently lower Wendy to the floor, covered in white sheets and cushions, you think contentedly that while there's plenty you don't know about Wendy Lake, you're looking forward to finding it all out.

But you'll be happy to fuck her, here among her old lovers and friends, who are all happily fucking themselves. This isn't the sort of party you ever expected to be at, or the sort of woman you'd ever planned on being with, but you can't imagine a happier place to end up.

THE END

"I do want you. Of course I do." You go on quickly—you don't want to get her hopes up. Despite everything, you don't want to hurt her. Not more than you have to. "But I don't think that would be a good idea. Us, I mean. I don't think it would work." You still care about Sarah, you still lust after Sarah—but you can't bring yourself to start dating her again, to get back into that cycle. And after finding her with that man, you don't think you could ever trust her again.

Sarah is still for a moment, then she pulls her hand from yours, back to clasp her drink. She finishes it just as the waitress brings her a refill and one for you. "I understand, Mark." She pulls the second drink toward her, takes a sip. "Listen, would you mind if we cut this short? I think I'd rather be alone if that's okay."

"Sure, of course." You're getting up, not sure what to do about your drink. You make a gesture toward it, but she cuts you off.

"Don't worry about that. I'll take care of it."

"Sarah—" You're worried about her, not sure if you should leave her alone here.

She sighs. "Mark, I'll be fine. Just go, okay? Please." She glances up, catches your eyes for a brief second before turning back to her glass.

What can you do? You go, you walk toward the exit. At the entrance to the room, you pause, look back. You expect to see Sarah alone, gulping down her drink, but two tall, good-looking Russian men are leaning over her table, flirting with her already. One starts to slide into the booth. She's smiling at him. The other man pulls over a chair, sits, and bends toward her. It's clear that Sarah won't lack for company tonight.

You take the subway home alone, wondering if you've made the right choice. One way or another, it's over. You'll go to work the next morning alone. You'll come home alone. Maybe someday you'll meet another woman, one who can actually make you happy. Or maybe you already met her and lost her. You've made your choice; all you can do is live with it.

THE END

You wake up the next morning in the tiny apartment where you live. There is a single slim window in the bedroom letting in light—not much, since it opens onto an airshaft and claustrophobic views of your neighbors across the way and the piles of trash on the ground three floors below. You live with battered wood floors and peeling wallpaper, a kitchen barely large enough to cook ramen in, and a bathroom without a tub. In what passes for a living room, you have one splintering desk pushed up against another slender, sealed-shut window, and a single metal folding chair. Your books are stacked across the floor; there's no room for bookcases, even if you could afford them. You found this place because a friend passed it on to you, and it's still hurting you— undergrad student loans are eating up $400 a month, and rent here is $1,050. You've never lived in a place this small before. You can hear rats in the walls at night.

You keep telling yourself it's only for a year. It's a one-year appointment; if they put you on tenure track, your pay will go up. It all depends on what you get done this year—what you research, what you publish. You were doing so well last year; two publications in your final year of grad school, good enough to get you several job offers. You could have taken a tenure-track job at some small school, could have stayed in Chicago. But you'd wanted to test yourself, to get the best job you could, which meant taking this position and then working like a dog to publish something decent. It's the chance to be a real academic, to do something serious, worthwhile.

Sarah didn't understand that—or if she did, she didn't care. She said all the hours with the books were what made her lose interest in you, in sex with you. She felt like she didn't know you anymore. You certainly didn't know her anymore. The girl you loved never would have picked up some stranger in a bar and brought him home to fuck on your living room couch.

You walked home from campus that day, along 57th Street to Kimbark, enjoying the fine spring weather. You resisted the urge to cross the street, to stop at 57th Street Books and browse for a while. You'd left campus early so that you could spend more time with Sarah. You climbed the stairs to the third-floor brownstone apartment you shared with her. Now, *that* was an apartment—back porch, large kitchen, dining room, bedroom, living room, front porch. You'd been planning to head for the kitchen, expecting to find Sarah there starting dinner. But when you opened the door, you heard noises from the living room, to your right. You walked down the hall, into the room. And there they were. You stood and watched them, wondering how you possibly could have messed up so badly that she would do this to you.

She was wearing a pink dress—the skirt of it was pushed up, bright against the dark brown leather of the couch that once had belonged to your grandmother. Most of her body was hidden by his, but you could see the skirt of her pink dress and her bare arms wrapped around his body, bare legs around his legs, her dusty heels pressing against his thighs, leaving smears of sweaty dirt. She refused to wear shoes or socks indoors, and the hardwood floors hoarded dust. You stared at the sideways line of Sarah's arched feet, digging into his thighs, as she whimpered, hidden behind his body. You knew you should do something—shout, throw something, walk away, slam the door. But you couldn't move. It had been so long since you'd heard her make those sounds. Your chest felt tight and your head was pounding and you stood there, watching them fuck, listening to her moan, for minutes that stretched into hours, into days.

116

Sarah's long legs wrapped around him, his ass bobbing up and down, pumping away. You can't get that image out of your head—and every time it pops up, it turns you on. It turns you on now. You spit in your hand and grab your cock; you masturbate quickly, imagining the stranger's ass slamming into your girlfriend. It's an image you've jerked off to all summer, but today it changes. Sarah's short blond hair turns long, silky black. Her pink summer dress turns ice blue. It's your ass bobbing up and down, your cock pounding into her. And she's silent, she's biting her lip and taking it as you fuck her, fuck her hard and fast until you come, spurting all over your chest.

You shower, dress, and go to teach your class.

• PLEASE TURN TO PAGE 46.

Wendy has three rules, as far as you can tell. You never get to question her instructions. You never get to give her instructions yourself. And, of course, you never get to spend the night. When you push her on any of these, she gets angry and doesn't call you for days. You find yourself waiting obsessively by the phone in your cramped apartment, hunched over in your single chair, eyes closed, fantasizing about fucking Wendy in her huge bed, in that apartment with the high ceilings and echoing spaces. When you can't stand the waiting anymore, you go to the university gym, pumping iron until your arms are trembling, or running blindly on the track. Pretty young coeds flirt with you, but you can't bring yourself to care about them. You're living for Wendy's phone call, for the moment when she'll invite you back.

It's humiliating, when you stop and think about it. So you don't let yourself think—you just live in your body. You eat, you sleep, you work out, you jerk off, and, when Wendy lets you, you fuck her. Sometimes, when you've pleased her, there are other women. The first time she brought another women into her bed with you, you'd expected to be excited. But you found instead that you couldn't bring yourself to care—even though Maggie, a voluptuous redhead, was quite attractive. You couldn't even get hard for her; only when Wendy brushed against you, bent down, and licked your ear, did your cock rise up. You fucked the redhead then, and other women on other nights. A slender Japanese woman, Yumiko. A pair of blond twins. Wendy likes to watch you fucking them, her hand between her thighs, slowly moving in and out, while you fuck the women across the bed, up against the wall. You fuck them as well as you can, knowing that afterward you'll get to fuck Wendy again.

The night after the blondes come over, when you and Wendy are lying side by side in bed after sex, you can't hold it in anymore. You have to know: if she's bringing other people into bed with you both, does that mean she's seeing other people at other times, too? On those nights when she doesn't call you, is she sitting at home working, or is she off fucking them?

"Wendy?"

"Yes, Mark?"

You hesitate; it's dangerous asking this kind of question. She won't like it. And, in fact, you're not even sure what to ask. You want to know where you stand—is this a relationship, or is it something else? Does she care about you at all, or is she playing with you? That's too hard to ask, though. It's easier to ask a question with a simple, factual answer: "Are you seeing anybody else?" Even thinking about the possibility makes your head pound.

Wendy slides up on an elbow; the moonlight is behind her, casting shadows across her face. "You mean, am I fucking anybody else?" Her voice is utterly calm.

"Yes." She must be able to see everything on your face, turned toward hers. You almost wish you hadn't asked the question—you're sure you won't like the answer. Your stomach feels twisted.

"Yes." She says it so calmly.

"Does that mean I get to have sex with other people, too?" You know the answer to this question, but you have to ask, have to hear her say it, how unfair this is.

"No. You're mine. Your cock, your ass, your sweet mouth. Remember?" Wendy smiles. She doesn't say anything else—just watches you, curiously.

You don't know what to do next. Part of you wants to grab her arms and shake her until she breaks down, tells you that she's sorry, that she'll never fuck anyone else again. But what right do you have to get angry? Wendy never promised to be faithful to you—all she ever promised was that she'd keep fucking you, and fuck you well. You can't claim she hasn't kept her word on that. So, even though there's a pit of fear and frustration in your belly, you can't do a damn thing about it.

Well, you could leave. Just get up and go. Never see her again outside the department, never sleep with her again. You'd meet somebody else, someday. You'd have a normal relationship, with a normal girl who wouldn't tell you what to do.

Is that what you want? Or do you want Wendy Lake, on whatever terms she'll give you?

• *If you choose to walk out,* PLEASE TURN TO PAGE 105.

• *If you choose to stay,* PLEASE TURN TO PAGE 55.

You fly first-class, of course. The food isn't good, but it's edible; usually you have to bring along a sandwich when you fly. And the seats are incredibly comfortable. Each one has its own private TV screen built into the chair in front, with a separate selection of movies to choose from—you could get used to traveling like this! The only drawback is that the first-class rest room is in front of you, extremely visible to everyone else in the compartment. You'd had fantasies of sneaking into it with Wendy, becoming members of the mile-high club, but it's too damn conspicuous. You content yourself with draping a blanket over both your laps, reaching under it to push up her long, loose skirt, finding her naked pussy underneath and playing with it, sliding your fingers in and out, slowly, brushing gently against her clit. Wendy reads a novel throughout, seeming utterly unmoved—but her cunt pulses around your fingers, and her wetness coats your fingers. It's a good way to pass the time on the long flight.

When you arrive at the hotel, the Acropolis Palace, you're startled by its opulence.

"This is a conference hotel?" You've been to classics conferences—inevitably, they choose the dingiest hotel in the area in order to keep costs affordable for professors on limited travel budgets.

Wendy actually blushes. "Well, they offered to pay for my room at the conference hotel. I told you that. But I couldn't bring myself to stay there—we'll be much more comfortable here. And I know the staff here . . . it's where I always stay."

"I see." And you do, as first the bellhops, then the concierge, then the elevator man all flirt outrageously with Wendy.

"Koukla, pame spiti mou?"

"Se agapo!"

"Moromou!"

She laughs in response and smooches her lips at the bellhops, calling back, *"Afgadhisto!"* You don't understand what anyone's saying, but the intent is clear. They all want her, which is nice for her but uncomfortable for you. You can't blame them, though—Wendy is stunning in a slim white dress and white sandals, perfect for the weather, which the concierge informs you is unseasonably warm. It feels like it's almost seventy degrees; if it stays like this, you won't be needing the sweaters you packed.

You have a quick dinner, then collapse—you're both too exhausted from the day's long flight to do much else. You wake up in the morning, roll out of bed, and walk over to open the curtains and windows; bright sun shafts in from a perfect blue sky. In New York, you'd be walking to campus in gray autumnal weather; today someone else is covering your class (through Wendy's intercession), and you're free to spend the day sight-seeing.

Wendy comes up behind you, tying a robe around her body.

"So, what's on the itinerary for today—the Parthenon?" You can't wait to see that, to walk on the grassy Acropolis, to stand against the towering pillars.

She smiles and asks, "Would you mind going to that tomorrow, when I'm prepping for my talk? I've seen it a hundred times—I'd like to take you someplace special."

"I'm at your command, milady." You grin and sketch her a mock bow.

She laughs. "Now, that's what I like to hear." Wendy seems different here in Athens. Happier, more relaxed. Maybe it's the weather, maybe it's just being in Greece. Home of the philosophers: Aristotle, Socrates, Plato, Xenocrates; the physicians: Hippocrates and Galen; the playwrights: Sophocles, Euripides, Aristophanes; the historians:

Herodotus and Thucydides; and, of course, home of Homer, whose *Odyssey* is still one of your favorite stories ever.

You're astonished that you're here. You feel dizzy, euphoric. You pull Wendy into your arms and kiss her—hard, passionately. She seems startled, but after a moment, she starts kissing you back, her arms coming up around your neck, her hands lacing themselves into your hair. Your cock grows hard against her thigh, but Wendy pulls away, laughing.

"There's a car and driver waiting downstairs, and the site closes at three, so go shower! By yourself! We'll have time for that sort of thing later."

"Wendy—" you start to protest, but she looks sternly at you until you can't help laughing. You concede defeat. "Yes, Milady," you say meekly, and go off to shower. Later had better come soon.

Your destination turns out to be about an hour's drive from Athens, the temple of Artemis at Vravrona, also known as the Parthenon of the Bear Maidens. Any residual crankiness you may have been feeling at being deprived of morning sex dissolves when you arrive at the site—elegant marble pillars situated at the foot of a prehistoric hill fort. You climb out of the car and follow Wendy to the site. Some of the pillars are partially submerged in water, some are dry, but they're all beautiful and convey a sense of quiet and peace.

You walk among the pillars for a while, until you end up a short distance away, looking at them, thinking about how old they are, how long they've endured. Wendy comes up and slips into your arms, leaning her back against your chest, looking out over the stones and water. You wrap your arms under her breasts, and she interlaces her arms with yours. "I try to make it out here whenever I come to

Greece," she says quietly. "I've always come alone before." She turns her head and smiles impishly at you. "Men aren't supposed to come here—it's a place for female worship."

You can't help being touched, knowing that you're the first man she's brought here; you tighten your arms briefly around her. "I've heard of this place, I think." Your Greek knowledge isn't as strong as it ought to be, but you do remember some things from grad school. "Wasn't Iphigenia supposedly sacrificed here before the Trojan wars?" You can't imagine someone being killed here—blood on the stones. It's such a peaceful place.

Wendy nods. "Sort of. She was the priestess here. She wasn't actually killed, but she did sacrifice her life to the service of the goddess. The initiates here had to handle all kinds of dangers—marauding invaders from the east, Persians, pirates, Ionian islanders, and severe flooding that drove them away from the temple for good. It wasn't easy, being a priestess of Artemis." She sounds wistful at the thought.

"But you would have loved it." It's a guess, but you can tell there's something here that calls to her.

Wendy's fingers gently caress yours. It's an unusually affectionate gesture for her, and it makes you feel close to her, protective. "It's crazy, I know, but I think I would have. Artemis was all about dualities—life and death, peace and war, marriage and virginity, even being tamed and untamed. When you worship Artemis, you don't have to choose one or the other, you can have both. You can have all the choices at once." She chuckles. "That may not have been perfect temple doctrine, but it's how I choose to interpret it. I also like the idea of young Athenian girls dressing up as bear cubs. I would have made a good bear."

"I'm sure you would have." You drop a kiss on top of her head. Later, you'll take her back to the hotel, you'll make love in the bed that's almost as big as the one she has at home. For now, you're content to stand here, enjoying a moment of communion, of peace.

The next morning, you wake early. Wendy is sleeping soundly, so you wash and dress quietly, leaving her a note. *Went to the Parthenon—back around 4.* That'll give her plenty of time to prepare for her talk, and still let you share some lazy afternoon sex before dinner and the presentation.

You walk for hours on the Acropolis. The Parthenon is immense, majestic—it's astonishing that it has survived the passage of years so well. You visit the two other temples of Athena, then make your way down the slope to the Theater of Dionysius. You sit on the stones and eat a gyro sandwich for lunch; you imagine Aristophanes there as well, watching as actors rehearsed his *Lysistrata*. It's *Lysistrata* that sends you back to the hotel early—the thought of all those poor Athenian men being denied sex by their heartless wives is too much for your libido. You miss Wendy. You've given her enough time to prepare for her talk.

You come back up to your room, unlock the door, and step inside, saying, "I decided to come back early."

"I can see that," Wendy says calmly. She's lying on the bed, still wearing the robe from breakfast. Less calm is the slender bellhop, barely more than a boy, who scrambles off the bed, grabs his pants, and ducks out the door, muttering feverishly in Greek. Apologies, presumably. Not that you care what he has to say.

"What's going on here?" You're proud of yourself for keeping your voice calm, but it's not as calm as Wendy's as she asks, "Do you want details?"

Your calm disappears. "No, I don't want any fucking details!"

"Oh, good, so you do know what was going on." Her tone is light, sardonic.

"Dammit, Wendy." Why is she doing this to you? Things had been going so well; you'd started to feel like you could trust her.

Wendy rises from the bed, tying the robe closed around her body. "Mark, we never promised to be monogamous. Stavros is an old friend of mine."

"He's barely old enough to be able to find his dick!"

She shrugs carelessly. "Now you're being petty."

You take a step forward into the room. "Wendy, I thought we had something pretty good going here. This last week, yesterday . . . yesterday was perfect." Your chest is tight—you don't want to lose her. But you have to say the rest of it: "I can't be with you if you're going to be screwing around with random guys whenever I'm not here."

Wendy's face is impassive, her eyes dark. You can't read her at all. "You can always leave, Mark. Pay for your own hotel room. Fly back tomorrow. Nothing says you have to stick around."

Before you were hurt, now you're hurt and angry. She's acting like you don't matter to her at all. "Is that it? Either I put up with this or I leave? I don't have any other options?"

For the first time in this dialogue, Wendy hesitates. "Honestly, I don't know." You expect her to continue, but she falls silent instead. The silence stretches out, filling the room.

• *If you go find another hotel room and then go home*, PLEASE TURN TO PAGE 41.

• *If you stay and keep talking to Wendy*, PLEASE TURN TO PAGE 91.

All of a sudden, you're not that turned on anymore. This doesn't feel right, using your relationship as fodder for a sex game. There is something real between the two of you. Well, at least you hope there is.

You look her in the eyes and say quietly, "I'd rather not." And then you wait to see what happens next.

Wendy's eyes narrow, and for a second, you think she's about to explode. You've never seen her actually angry, she's always in control. Even if it ruins your life, it would be an interesting way to go. But, after a moment, she starts laughing quietly.

"Oh, Mark. You're always surprising me, my dear. Of course, if you don't want to, you needn't. It was just a silly bet."

You appear to have gotten away with refusing her. What you'd like to do now is go somewhere and fuck her brains out, but she needs to save face in front of her friends. You don't need to ask how. You don't even need to wait for her to explain. With a sly grin, you volunteer the seven words you know will make your mistress happy. Happy with you.

"I'd like to eat you, please, Mistress."

Wendy reaches out and ruffles your hair, chuckling. "Of course you can, sweet Mark. You go right ahead." She reaches down and pulls the black silk skirt up to her waist, baring her naked pussy. You slide to your knees and eagerly start lapping at her cunt. Your cock hardens, and your tongue moves faster.

You'll happily fuck her in front of this crowd all night long—and fuck her friends, too, if it makes her happy. What matters is that you know she does care about you, that it's not just sex or power games. Oh, it's those, too, of course. You love the sex and the power games, and you know she does as well. But it's also something more.

Your lips are covered with her wet scent, your knees are getting sore, and you feel utterly content. This isn't anything like the life you expected when you came to New York, but somehow you've found exactly what you need to be happy.

THE END

Y ou wonder what Kimmie is like, why they think you'd like her. "Sure, I'd be glad to come by." You have trouble imagining these people in a house, wearing clothes. It's a disconcerting thought.

"Great. Terrific. I'll give you the details before we leave." Rick grins widely, clearly delighted. "I'm pretty damn horny from sucking you off. I'd like to fuck my wife's ass, if it's okay with her. You can watch, if you like."

"It's definitely okay with me, baby," Rhonda says, smiling, clearly turned on herself.

You slide down to lean against the wall. You're too tired for much else, and you've never had anal sex yourself, or seen it live. Watching for a bit sounds like a good plan. Rhonda gets down on her hands and knees again; Rick slathers saliva on his cock, rubbing it until it's nice and hard. It's turning you on, watching his hand move on that immense cock. You spit on your own hand and lightly rub your own slightly sore cock. You're not trying to make yourself come—it's just nice to be sitting here, watching him stroke himself hard, then wet himself more before placing his cock against Rhonda's pink asshole.

She rests her chest and face against the floor, then reaches behind herself, puts her hands on her ass cheeks, and pulls them wide, opening herself up for him. Rick starts to push, slowly but firmly, into Rhonda's open ass. She winces slightly but pushes back against him anyway, urging him on. The head of his cock slides in with a small pop, and she yelps softly. Rick stops for a second, giving her time to get used to the sensation of being stretched open. Your cock is hard, and you wish it were you, pushing into Rhonda's wide ass. He pushes farther in then, bit by bit, until he's buried to the hilt. She's biting her lip, but when he starts to move, she moves with him, shoving back against him, groaning. Around you, the party continues, but this is plenty of entertainment.

As it turns out, that's all the action you get at the party; when you wander around later, you can't find the Indian girl; she seems to have left. And all the other women seem otherwise occupied. You watch Wendy being fucked by a very heavyset black man for a while. You expect it to bother you, but it doesn't, particularly. It's not arousing either, Wendy's pale thinness against his dark body; she seems so detached from it all. She was like that with you, too—all performance. Honestly, you find Rhonda sexier. Lots of enthusiasm, lots of great sounds. If her friend Kimmie is anything like her, you're sure you'll have fun tomorrow night. In fact, you should probably save your energy, and it's getting late. You dress and leave the party, nodding cordially at the doorman as you walk outside.

You walk back along Riverside Drive, moving in and out of the puddles of light cast by the streetlamps. Above your head, the last leaves on the trees are rustling in the chilly air—winter is coming, but your life isn't shutting down, it's opening up, filling with new options, with surprising twists and turns. You feel invigorated, rejuvenated; you walk faster, almost running down the street, looking forward to the morning and all its fascinating possibilities.

• PLEASE TURN TO PAGE 96.

"Look, I'm not going to agree without knowing what you're planning to do. I'm not an idiot, Wendy." Is that so hard for her to understand?

She shrugs. "I hadn't decided what I was going to do to you, actually. I was thinking about sticking a few of my fingers up your ass—or maybe getting down on my knees and sucking you off."

You take a step forward, your cock twitching. The idea of her on her knees, her mouth busy against your crotch, is incredibly arousing. "I don't know about that first option, but the second one sounds fine to me—let's just take it somewhere else. Your apartment or mine?"

Wendy sits down at her desk, picks up a pair of gold-rimmed glasses from the desk, and puts them on. They perch sexily on her nose. "Forget it, Mark. You lost your chance when you said no. I'm not interested anymore." She looks down at her papers, starts to shuffle through them. She says absently, "Now you'll never know what you and I could have done together."

"That's it?" You can't believe it—can she really be so capricious?

"That's it." She doesn't bother to look up.

"Fine." You unlock the door and open it, walk out, close it behind you. A student is standing there, waiting patiently for office hours to start. God, what if you'd gone along with Wendy, done whatever she wanted to do? This girl would've been standing outside the whole time. You walk quickly past the student, collect your things, and go home. You don't need this kind of craziness in your life, no matter how sexy Wendy might be.

• PLEASE TURN TO PAGE 132.

You buy the pill, pop it into your mouth, wrap your arms around your legs again, and wait. The boy disappears into the crowd. Indira comes back; she doesn't look nearly as pretty. You like her, but you're not crazy about her. You want it back, the sensation of being happy, joyous, in love even. It felt so good, so right. But it's not coming back. You're kissing her, sliding your hands under her shirt, rubbing her breasts with your fingers, and all you feel is your pulse pounding, your heart hammering in your chest. Your mouth is dry; the music's so loud, and you feel like you can't breathe. You try to breathe through her mouth, you squeeze her breasts, hard, and she gasps. She pulls away, out of your reach.

You stretch out a hand toward her, wanting to apologize, but you can't get the words out. Your heart is racing; everything looks blurry, and your legs are buckling underneath you. You're falling to the ground. You can't see Indira anymore, but you can hear her voice, hear other voices. *Shit, what did he take? I don't know, I don't know! He must've taken something while I was gone, something I didn't see, didn't test. Fuck, he's convulsing, you gotta call an ambulance! Get him out of here!* And there are hands underneath you, lifting you up, carrying you out of the building, propping you against the building wall. You can hear the sirens screaming, the sound pulsing through your head, sending your limbs jerking, your head slamming up against the brick wall, and everything's bright, sparkling, and then it all goes dark, darker than it's ever been before, and it's over, it's done, you've reached—

THE END

You can't help noticing that the department is less exciting without the Wendy Lake possibilities; women aren't walking up to you and asking you to fuck them in their offices. You wonder if maybe you made a mistake, not taking her up on her challenge. You don't want to get tangled with Wendy again—she was too domineering, too antagonistic. But your encounters with Wendy have aroused your libido; after long months of comfortable abstinence, you're waking up horny and continuing that way all day. You need to find a woman—someone beautiful, smart, and sane. New York must be full of women like that. How hard can it be to find one?

On Thursday, you attend a lecture on the role of medieval nuns in the Church. It's closely related to your own research, and one speaker's points start you thinking about your thesis work again. By the end of the lecture, you're feeling invigorated, and it didn't hurt that the talk was given by Belinda Lundstrom, an attractive brunette in a white blouse and gray skirt. Tailored, professional, smart.

You go up afterward and speak to her; she's even more interesting in person. It's exhilarating, talking to an attractive woman in your own field. You could never discuss your work with Sarah—she wasn't interested. And Wendy was much more interested in sex than in the ancient Greeks and Romans. Belinda obviously cares about her work—and she's familiar with your work, too, which is flattering. The conversation goes on and on, until everyone else has left the lecture room, leaving you two alone.

You think she's enjoying talking to you—it's hard to tell. At times Belinda looks melancholy, almost sad. She looks like she could use some cheering up. But she does get excited about her work, and you notice that her eyes sparkle when she's being enthusiastic; it's charming. It makes you want to try to make her smile; there's an appealing challenge to it. Belinda smells nice, too; sort of fruity. Her lips are full: they look soft, kissable.

You glance down at her hand—no wedding ring, although there's a tan line on the appropriate finger. Divorced? You're not sure, but it couldn't hurt to ask her out. It's been a long time since you actually asked a woman out—over six years, in fact. You take a deep breath.

"Belinda, I need to get going, but I'd like to keep talking about this. Do you want to have coffee sometime? Maybe on Sunday?" Coffee is low-key, nice and safe. This could be a purely academic discussion, just some colleagues getting together. Somehow you've gotten the impression that Belinda wouldn't respond well to outright flirting—better to take it slow, keep the pressure off.

Even so, she hesitates before answering. You almost expect her to say no. But she doesn't. "Sure, Mark. That would be fun. I'd enjoy that."

"Great!" You try not to sound too enthusiastic, but you feel triumphant, as if you've won something. You think it's not so easy, getting Belinda Lundstrom to go out with a guy.

You make plans to meet on Sunday before heading home. You whistle quietly as you walk uptown, thinking about Belinda's gentle voice, those soft lips. This should be interesting.

• PLEASE TURN TO PAGE 50.

You take the subway home, even though it's close enough to walk. You feel tired, worn out. You're melancholy, sorry for yourself, and the dingy gray subway surroundings, the grubby walls, and the lingering smell of piss only serve to underscore how less than fabulous your life currently is. You miss Chicago, and more than that, you miss having a girlfriend—the regular sex, the companionship. Having someone waiting when you get home, someone you can tell about your day. You're going home now to an empty, ugly apartment. You keep it neat, but that's not enough to make it someplace you're happy to come home to. When you get off the subway car, a young woman carrying a baby asks if you can spare some change. You fish out a dollar and hand it to her, hoping it makes her life better. You wish someone could do the same for you.

When you get inside your apartment, there's a message waiting on your machine.

"Hey, Mark—it's Sarah. I'm in New York on business. Do you want to meet up for drinks? I'm staying with a friend near Times Square. I'll be free tonight around nine. Call me on my cell if you want to meet up. Hope everything's good with you. Bye!"

She sounds so light, friendly, relaxed. She sounds happy. Your own life is a mess. Do you want Sarah to see you like this? Do you call her?

- *If you call Sarah,* PLEASE TURN TO PAGE 140.

- *If you don't call,* PLEASE TURN TO PAGE 228.

That night, you can't work. You're just waiting, waiting until it's time to go to Wendy's, time to find out what she has planned for you next. So you start to masturbate—you sit naked on your bed, your hand moving on your cock, jerking slowly up and down. The familiar scene of Sarah and the guy on your couch starts to play itself in your mind's eye—but again, it's Wendy instead of Sarah, and when you enter the room and pull down your pants, Wendy takes the guy's dick out of her pussy. You're kneeling on the floor, and she's leading his dick toward your ass, and you're willing your mind to stop. You're not queer, but the scene keeps playing out, inexorably. Your ass is high in the air, it's tingling, you're shivering with the visceral memory of this afternoon and with anticipation at the thought of taking more, taking a huge, thick dick inside you, of being fucked, hard and fast. Your hand moves faster and faster, and it isn't long before you come all over your hand.

Afterward, you get dressed for Wendy. It's strange, pulling on pants without underwear. Everything is hanging there, jostling around as you move. It's not exactly uncomfortable—in fact, it might even be more physically comfortable than underwear. But it feels strange. You can't help being very aware of your cock and balls as you walk west, over to her apartment on Riverside Drive; the lack of underwear makes you think about sex even more often than you normally do.

Wendy lives in an elegant part of town—pre-war buildings, beautifully designed, with arches, gargoyles, attractive facades. The streets are tree-lined, and in this pleasant weather, plenty of people are out and about, just strolling, enjoying the neighborhood. You hate to think what a place here must cost; something outrageous, you're sure. Her books must be selling very well, indeed.

A doorman greets you in the marble lobby, uniformed and epauletted, with a jaunty hat perched on his balding, egg-shaped head. He takes your name with an oddly penetrating look; he seems to be memorizing your face. How many men has he sent up to Wendy's apartment? The elevator takes you up to the penthouse floor, opening directly into her apartment. You walk through a short hallway, past a few doors, and into an open room, and then stop, staring. You don't want to look like some poor hick, but this place is like something out of a magazine. You didn't know people actually lived like this.

It's almost bare, at first glance. A huge, open space with high ceilings. It's the largest room you've seen in New York, even at the university. The amount of money this much space implies seems almost obscene. And this is only a single room—another living space is visible on the right, and an arched hallway leads left. The room has a few chairs upholstered in jewel-tone leathers. Green. Purple. Red. A massive painting hangs on one brick wall—naked figures entangled in a Dalíesque landscape in shades of blue. The effect is overwhelming.

Wendy is nowhere to be seen. You step farther into the room, looking more closely at the details. Somehow, you have no doubt that she did all this herself—there is no decorator's hand in it. What kind of woman would create a space like this? It's intense, beautiful, but hardly comfortable. You notice more erotic art. Nothing you recognize—they all seem to be original pieces. An ebony sculpture of a naked kneeling woman in one corner, her head thrown back, her wrists bound behind her. A statue of Pan, lewd, ecstatic, driving his cock into a goat. Small paintings hide in unexpected corners of the two main rooms—the second room is almost as large as the first, with a single steel table running the length of it and one tall chair at its head. Wendy apparently prefers to dine alone.

"So, do you like it?"

You turn. She's in the arch of the hallway, smiling, clearly pleased at your reaction. Wendy is naked. Her breasts are smaller than you expected, with dark pink aureoles. Her cunt hair looks silky, dark. At this point, you couldn't care less about her apartment or her art. You just want to have your hands on her bare flesh. You want to touch her, to try to please her. You want to fuck her again, hard, until she's screaming. But most of all, you want to do what she wants you to do. It's strange knowing that. It's not what you ever would have anticipated.

"Does it matter if I like it?"

"Not really." She turns then, walks down the hall. You cross the two rooms and follow her, your eyes locked on the gentle sway of her curving ass.

Her bedroom is different. Still large and mostly empty, but softer in design. Tall wooden shutters cross the length of one wall; they're pulled open, letting in a flood of moonlight across the bed. The bed itself is huge, even larger than king-size. It's covered in shades of silver, soft, silken fabrics. She takes your hand and pulls you onto the bed, rolling so you're underneath her. She unbuttons your shirt, pulls it off you, reaches to undo your pants. You try to help, but your hands get in her way—she pushes them aside, and so you lie there, letting her strip you naked.

When you're both naked, she turns and kneels above you, facing away. You've never been in this position before, but you're not about to object. The moonlight casts strange shadows on the curves of her body, where her neck meets her shoulder, where the base of her spine hits the curve of her ass. She reaches down and cups your balls in one hand, pulling them up. You feel a shiver of anticipation surge through you—you know what she's about to do. Wendy licks a finger on her other hand and then slides it underneath you. She's gentle this time, slow. She gives you time to appreciate the sensations, moving the finger in and out, just an inch, slowly. It's a strange, shivery sensation, but a good one. It makes all the skin on your body feel electrified; you think you can hear your pounding heart.

Your cock is sticking straight up, and Wendy starts rubbing her wet cunt against the tip. At first, she seems to be rubbing you against her clit; then she shifts, sliding you up against the opening to her pussy. She slides down an inch and then pulls back again. Up and down, a bit at a time, while her finger slides in and out of your ass. You take it as long as you can, but finally, you can't stand it anymore. You don't know if she'll be angry, but you don't care— you can't help yourself. You grab her hips and pull her down onto your cock, all the way, slamming your hips up, driving deep inside her. Wendy groans then and shoves another finger deep into your ass. It hurts, but you don't care. You fuck her, your eyes open, watching her ass bounce up and down as she squeezes your balls and finger-fucks your ass, and it's not long before you're coming, coming hard, shooting into her.

She pulls herself off you, turns on the bed to face you. Wendy shakes her head. "You came too quickly for me."

You feel a quick flush of shame. It's been a long time since a woman complained about that—you thought you were past that kind of thing. You need to pay more attention if you want to keep up with this woman. "I'm sorry. What would you like me to do for you?"

"I'd like you to lick this finger." Wendy is holding out a finger, smiling. Presumably, one of the fingers that a minute ago was buried in your ass. Your stomach does a quick flip, and your gorge rises. You don't want to do this—but she wants you to. You know you won't enjoy this. Are you willing to do it anyway, because it will please her?

- *If you lick the finger,* PLEASE TURN TO PAGE 86.

- *If you find the idea repulsive and refuse,* PLEASE TURN TO PAGE 52.

Y ou call Sarah—she wants you to come down to Times Square, to meet up at the Russian Vodka Room for drinks. You agree. You hang up the phone, still smiling from the sound of her voice. It reminds you of all the other times you met for dinner when you were first going out. All the dinners you ate together in your apartment. So many good evenings spent together.

When you get to the restaurant, Sarah's already there, in a small booth in the far corner. She rises to greet you; you almost don't recognize her. She's done something to her hair—streaked the blond with red? It's grown some; it's brushing against her bare shoulders as she walks. She has a nice tan. She's lost some weight, too; in fact, in those thigh-high black boots and a short spaghetti-strap dress, she looks hotter than you've ever seen her, and your cock shifts in your pants. Apparently, breaking up with you was good for Sarah.

You hug her hello, and your hands instinctively curve around to the small of her back, where they rested so often before. Her head fits just under your chin, and her hair smells like sunshine, even in the crowded, smoky room. You've barely touched her, and already your cock is hard, ready—your body remembers what it was like, holding her, fucking her. Your body wants to do it again.

She tilts her head up a little. "Hey," she says softly. Her breath is soft against your neck, and you fight to repress a shiver. You don't want her to know how she's affecting you.

You keep your voice even, friendly. "Hey, yourself. It's good to see you."

"You, too." Sarah lingers there a moment longer, then pulls away. You let her go reluctantly. You could have held her like that for a long time. Instead, she slides into the booth, and you slide in next to her. Her thigh is pressed warmly against yours; you're grateful for the crowded room making it so easy to touch her. You wonder if there's any chance she'd be up for a quickie at your apartment before she goes back to Chicago. Maybe that's why she wanted to get together. She used to like having sex with you.

"So, any idea what's good here?" you ask.

"Alex said to order the caviar-topped blinis. And lots of other stuff. It's sort of like a tapas bar—lots of small plates. Get whatever you like; it's on me." Before you can protest, she continues, "Or rather, on the magazine. They're paying for this trip." She hesitates, takes a sip of her pale green martini. Then says, "They gave me a promotion to senior editor—and they want me to move to New York."

"Well, that's certainly news." You know you should be happy for her, congratulate her on the promotion, but you're too stunned.

Sarah's voice turns sharp. "Does it bother you? That I might move to New York?"

"Why would it bother me?" Your own voice is utterly flat.

"Come on, Mark. Be honest with me. The last thing I want to do is hurt you." She's bent over the drink, her hands curved around the glass, sipping it calmly.

And suddenly you can't be calm; there's a flash of anger burning right through you. "Oh, really? I'm sure that thought was uppermost in your mind when I caught you fucking that bastard on my grand-mother's couch." You spit the words out, wanting to hurt her, too.

Sarah's hand jerks, spilling a little of the drink. "I said I was sorry. I said it a hundred, a thousand times. It was a stupid thing to do, and I did it for stupid reasons, and I wish I could take it back, but I can't." Her voice is trembling, and tears are welling in her eyes.

"What more do you want from me? Christ! This was a bad idea. I shouldn't have come." She's rising from the table, but she's trapped in the corner; she can't get out unless you stand, too.

You reach out, take her arm. "No, Sarah—wait. Wait. I'm sorry, too, okay? Don't go, please." You didn't mean to make her cry; or maybe you did, just a little. But you're satisfied, and you don't want her to go. You're not ready to say good-bye to her yet. You tug at her arm, willing her to sit. "Stay." After a moment, she sinks back down into the booth.

"So," she says in a small voice. "You don't mind about the move?"

You shrug. "No. I don't think so. I don't know. Let me think about it a minute, okay?"

"Okay." She takes a deep breath and picks up the menu, biting her lip. She always bites her lip when she's thinking—and it always makes you want to kiss her and then bite her lip yourself. Every damn time.

You pick up Sarah's drink and take a sip, trying to buy some time to think. It doesn't taste like alcohol at all—it tastes like green apples. Strange.

Sarah in New York: it's hard to imagine. You'd always thought of her as a stay-at-home girl, but she looks entirely at ease here in the midst of this smoky bar, casually chatting with the waitress who comes to take your order. *What do you recommend? Pickled herring— you're kidding! Maybe you should bring me another of these amazing drinks—and one for him, too. We're going to need a little longer.* A little longer sounds good. You're beginning to realize that there are aspects of Sarah you never knew about. Maybe that's your own fault—maybe you never made the effort to truly know her. Maybe it's not too late.

You try to sound casual as you ask, "So, are you going to take the job? Do you have a choice?"

Sarah shrugs. "Oh, I could stay in Chicago if I wanted to. It'd be better if I came to New York. But I don't know anybody here. It's scary, to be honest." She takes another sip of her drink. Her head is tipped down over the glass, her hair shading her face. You can't see her expression.

You reach out then, take her chin in your hand and tip it up into the light. "You know me." You still care about her; how could you not, after six years together? Maybe she wouldn't be up for the sex, but if she came here, you could at least be friends. You could spend time together, have dinners, go to the theater, go for walks in the park. It would be frustrating, but it would be better than nothing. You release her chin but reach over and take her free hand, squeezing it reassuringly.

Sarah looks at you steadily. She swallows before saying, "I wasn't sure if you'd be willing to even see me again. Much less anything else."

Anything else? Your heart thumps, and your hand tightens involuntarily on hers. "Sarah, do you want something else?" She'd refused to move with you; you'd thought she lost interest in you. If she hasn't . . .

Her voice drops, becomes softer. But her eyes stay steady on yours. "Mark, you asked me to move to New York with you. Even after that incident. I couldn't go then, I wasn't ready—but I can now. I still love you, still want you. The only question *I* have is whether you still want me."

Do you?

- *If you don't want her to come to New York*, PLEASE TURN TO PAGE 112.

- *If you invite Sarah to come to New York and move in with you*, PLEASE TURN TO THE NEXT PAGE.

Y ou can't believe you've gone this long without her. The following Friday afternoon, Sarah arrives for real. She takes a
cab from the airport, rings your buzzer. You buzz her up,
open the door, and wait. She comes up the stairs; you hold her tight,
drop kisses in her hair.

Sarah puts down her duffel bag as you close the door—then she's
in your arms, kissing you, and she's crying, but you know that the
tears don't mean to stop, they mean that she missed you. They make
you feel tender toward her, protective. She seems suddenly fragile.
So you kiss her. You kiss her lips and her cheeks and even her forehead.
You kiss away the tears; you kiss her neck, her shoulder. You walk
her to the bed, still kissing her. Her hands are busy on your shirt,
unbuttoning it.

The phone rings. You ignore it, unzipping her dress, sliding it
off. It rings again and again. The answering machine comes on.

"Mark, it's Wendy." Her voice is husky, low. "Are you there?"

Should you get that?" Sarah asks in a soft voice.

"Just a colleague," you say. Wendy's saying something about
calling her, but you ignore her. Sarah's wearing a black cotton bra
and panties—simple but sexy, especially against her pale gold skin.
And those boots. They're great boots, but you have no idea how to
get them off. Are you supposed to unlace them? Sarah solves that
problem for you, reaching down between her thighs to take hold of
a hidden zipper and unzip them—first the right, then the left. She
kicks them off. You peel off the long black socks covering her slender legs. She lies back on the bed, waiting, while you take off the
rest of your clothes. You love looking at her like this, waiting for
you; you love knowing that her nipples are hard under the cotton
bra, that her pussy is wet inside those panties. You bend down and

start kissing her again, but this time you start at her small feet and work your way up.

You kiss her ankle, her calf, the ticklish back of her knee. She squirms but doesn't stop you. You kiss her thighs, hear the intake of breath as you move farther up them. She's trembling a little, and something about that pleases you. You don't want to think about it too closely. Instead, you slide farther up, breathe gently against her panties. She shivers. You lick the fabric, tasting the faint tang of her through it. You lick until she's whimpering, arching her hips slightly against your mouth. Then you pull the fabric to one side and plant a wet kiss directly on her clit. She thrusts sharply against your mouth and lets out a small cry, almost as if you gave her an electric shock.

You lick her again and again, and you don't need to think about what to do; your tongue knows what will please her, what will make her moan and twist on the bed. Sarah's getting closer, her breath coming faster, her hips lifting rhythmically to meet your mouth. Closer and closer, until you reach up and squeeze her nipples through the cloth, and that does it, that sends her up and over the top, and she's coming hard against your wet mouth.

You pull the panties off. You move up the bed, reach underneath her, unhook her bra, and pull it off. You spread Sarah's legs with yours and sink your hard cock into her. It feels like coming home.

You spend the weekend getting reacquainted, kissing, talking, fooling around. Sarah seems excited about the move to New York. She has a fair bit of money saved up; she convinces you to move, and by the end of the following week, you've found a two-bedroom apartment in Brooklyn. It's smaller than your old place in Chicago, but it's a lot bigger and nicer than Harlem. One bedroom is set aside as your study—with Sarah there to make dinner again, you start to get some research done. More sex, better food, productive work—by the end of September, it's clear that in every way, Sarah's arrival has made your life better. This is what you'd originally hoped for when you took the job in New York. This is the life you wanted.

When you're not working, you explore the city together. Sarah loves art, so she takes you not just to the Met but also to the Brooklyn Museum of Art, which is much more impressive than you would have expected. You're more of a food person than an art person, so you spend time on the Web researching good restaurants to take her to—affordable but delicious. The Spumoni Gardens for pizza, or Grimaldi's. Italian rice balls at Joe's. Planet Thai on Bedford Avenue. Her favorite is Peruvian food at Coco Roco, where you both order the Argentine steak stir-fry every time you go; at under ten bucks each, it's impossible to resist.

Sarah is quickly becoming a New Yorker; you're not sure how you feel about that. She's changing, becoming more sharp and sparkly than she was in Chicago, but also more brittle somehow. She's still mostly Sarah, though, prone to sudden enthusiasms and intense attachments. In late October it's shoes in SoHo. Even with a job, she can't afford the shoes there—five hundred dollars easily for a pair of leather boots with sharply pointed toes. But she likes to look; she doesn't seem to find it frustrating, not being able to buy. It would drive you crazy if you were her, but since you're only along for the ride, you don't mind people-watching while Sarah tries on overpriced shoes. You're standing outside a store window, watching women buy fancy lingerie, when you see her. Wendy Lake. Inside the store, talking to a salesclerk, buying a delicate, sheer chemise. Her hair is loose, falling down in a long dark cascade, hiding her face. She can't see you watching her, so you watch a little longer. You can't help imagining what she might look like in that chemise; it's short enough that it would barely reach to mid-thigh. Wendy's long legs would extend out, stretching all the way to the floor—or they'd be spread-eagle on the bed.

Sarah steps out of a store a few doors down and calls to you. With a slight effort, you turn away from the image of Wendy and walk to join your girlfriend. You feel guilty, but you tell yourself that a man is allowed to look. And imagine.

After that, it seems like you see Wendy everywhere. On a beautiful Indian-summer day in early November, you take Sarah to Central Park for an impromptu picnic in Sheep's Meadow. You eat strawberries and drink champagne, but you're distracted from kissing Sarah when you catch a glimpse of Wendy Lake walking past you, dramatically elegant in a dark red dress, heading toward the Tavern on the Green. When you're ice-skating in the rink later that night, laughing with Sarah as she stumbles around the edge, Wendy whips past you, so fast that you catch just a glimpse of her profile before she disappears into the crowd.

You're not even sure it was her—as November ripens, it seems like you're seeing Wendy every time you turn around, but it's never actually her. Just other tall, dark-haired women, clicking by in heavy coats and pointy-toed boots. When you take Sarah to see *Chicago* in Times Square, you think you see Wendy at the theater, sitting a few rows ahead of you. You're sure it's her—all through the first act until, at intermission, the woman stands and turns toward the aisle. And it isn't Wendy, of course. You should have known better; you can't imagine Wendy Lake at a musical. And yet you thought it was her.

Maybe it's you. It must be you. You don't know why, but ever since that day in SoHo, you can't stop thinking about Wendy Lake. Dressed, half dressed, naked. But always turning to you, always inviting you to her office, her bedroom, to fuck, to suck, to do things you've never imagined doing. You have no reason to believe that Wendy is still interested in you and every reason to think she isn't. She ignores you in the department, on the occasions when your paths inevitably cross, at seminars, faculty meetings. She's always talking to someone else, someone who's listening intently to what she has to say, who's laughing at her jokes. She ignores you, and you tell yourself that's what you want, exactly how you want it to be.

After all, you have a girlfriend—you have Sarah. Sarah loves you, and it's not her fault that she can't offer escapades as intriguing, as dangerous, as delicious as your imagined exploits with Professor Lake.

You put Wendy out of your mind. It gets easier as the semester draws to an end—the last weeks of November and the first weeks of December are insanely busy. Your students are writing final papers, getting ready to take their exams. You're in office hours every single day, and when you're not, there's a rush of last-minute seminars and meetings to attend as everyone tries to wrap things up before the holidays. There are holiday parties, too—department shindigs that you're expected to attend. You take Sarah; she's a big hit with your colleagues. They think she's cute, funny, charming. And she is, of course. She is.

You introduce her to Wendy Lake at the last party of the year, the week before finals.

"So, this is the famous Sarah?" she says, unfolding her Chanel compact and applying lipstick while she talks. Somehow Wendy manages to be friendly and condescending at the same time. You don't think Sarah notices, though.

"It's so nice to meet you," Sarah says enthusiastically. "I enjoyed *Love Among the Ancients* tremendously. Do you have another book coming out soon?"

You're startled. You hadn't realized that Sarah has read Wendy's books. Sarah does read voraciously; it's part of her job as a magazine editor, and Wendy does write books geared toward a popular audience. Still, you feel embarrassed—you haven't read any of Wendy's books yourself.

Wendy arches an elegant eyebrow. "Not this year, I'm afraid. But I'm glad you're enjoying my work. Mark's lucky to have a partner who appreciates what we do—so many people think of classicists as boring old anachronisms."

"Oh, you could never be boring!" Sarah says. She smiles, looking very young and sweet. You realize that Sarah must be at least ten years younger than Wendy Lake. It's an odd realization.

"I am very lucky," you say. "But I'm afraid I have to steal Sarah away now—she hasn't met Professor Benjamin yet." You take Sarah's arm and start to draw her away.

Sarah reaches out and takes Wendy's hand. Her hand looks small and somehow defenseless, framed by Wendy's long, manicured fingers. "It was lovely meeting you, Professor Lake." You can't seem to stop looking at their hands intertwined.

Wendy smiles and squeezes Sarah's hand before letting go. "And you, my dear." You turn and walk away with your hand on Sarah's waist, guiding her through the crowd—but when you glance back, Wendy's still standing there, watching you both with an odd, speculative look in her eyes. You walk faster.

The next week is painfully harried. You hand in the last set of grades on Friday, finishing the semester, and then take the subway home in the early evening, enduring the shivering cold. You'd thought nothing could beat a frigid Chicago winter, but winter in New York has its own special miseries: slush and sleet and dampness that chill the bones. Your head is pounding—you think you might be getting a migraine. All you want is a cup of hot soup, some dry socks, and some peace and quiet to write up the insight that came to you while you were teaching.

You open the door to hear music playing—something classical, soft and mellow. It's startling: Sarah's supposed to be at work. What's going on? You follow the music to the bedroom. When you open the bedroom door, you see Sarah, naked on the bed, in the wash of candlelight. Her hair and skin look damp, as if she's just climbed out of the tub. The room smells like vanilla and roses. Your cock stirs briefly in your pants as Sarah smiles up at you.

"It's been a while since we fucked."

Has it? You've lost track; you've been so busy at work lately, and the cold has made you exhausted. You're tired now; Sarah looks good, she smells good, and part of you responds, but another part of you wants to curl up next to her and go to sleep.

It's the old problem again—this is why you broke up the first time. But this time she's not just complaining that you never want sex; she's trying to do something about it. How can you resist that?

• PLEASE TURN TO PAGE 154.

Y ou don't hear from Wendy the next day, or the one after that. It's three days later when she finally calls you, in your office. It isn't a pleasant call.

"Mark. You left my party early." She sounds irritated.

You get up and close the door; you don't want the department hearing this conversation. "It wasn't my kind of scene, Wendy. I'd much rather spend more time alone with you." You try to sound seductive, teasing. "Do you want to have dinner tonight? I've been thinking about what we might do for dessert—"

"Mark." Her voice has gotten cold. "I'm not interested in dessert. Frankly, I'm not interested in you anymore."

What? "You're going to drop me, just because I didn't stay at your party?" She's got to be kidding.

But Wendy says, "If you'd stayed, you might have learned something. Your horizons might have expanded. You live in a small world, Mark, a world that isn't big enough to hold me."

You cut her off then. There's only so much pompous lecturing you can take. "Whatever, Wendy. That's fine. Have a nice life." You slam the phone down and take a few deep breaths. You want to punch something.

Instead you write a note, *Office hours canceled today,* and stick it on your door. You grab your jacket and go home.

• PLEASE TURN TO PAGE 134.

Your phone becomes compelling—from the time you arrive home, at four, you keep turning to look at it. You want to call. But she said tonight, not this afternoon. You pull out your books and try to work; you wait through five, through six, through dinner, and then through seven. Finally, at seven-thirty, you put the books aside and call. You've waited long enough.

"Hello, Wendy."

"Mark. Now isn't a good time." Her voice sounds odd—slightly rough, ragged.

"Should I call back later?" Is that another woman's voice you're hearing in the background? Wendy takes a moment to respond.

"Maybe not tonight, sweet pea. Call me tomorrow." Her voice trails off into a gasp. You know what's going on—and that definitely is another woman's voice.

"Maybe I'll do that. Good-bye, Wendy."

"Mm-hmm . . ." And she hangs up.

Part of you is annoyed, but another part is intrigued. You sit in your armchair, undo your pants, take your dick in your hand. You stroke yourself slowly, imagining Wendy Lake naked in bed, trying to have a phone conversation while another woman squirms between her thighs, sucking her, finger-fucking her. If you have to get blown off, at least it's for a good cause. Still, do you want to keep dealing with this kind of thing? Invitations to blow jobs that dissipate into nothing; invitations to call that turn into sex with other people. Do you want to keep pursuing this erratic woman?

• If you call Wendy the next night, PLEASE TURN TO PAGE 177.

• If you decide not to bother, PLEASE TURN TO PAGE 37.

P rofessor Lake is wearing black today: a soft turtleneck sweater that outlines the gentle curves of her breasts, and slim, tailored black slacks. Very professional and not nearly as accessible as yesterday's outfit. It's just as well—the hallway is well traveled, with students and professors going back and forth during office hours. You can hear the muffled murmur of conversation through the closed door.

Wendy is standing behind her desk, near a large window overlooking the grassy lawns. It's quite an office she has here. She gazes at you speculatively, then says, "Close the door, and lock it."

You do, then turn back to her, wondering where she thinks this is going. You're having a hard time reading this woman. It's part of her appeal, but it's also frustrating. You have no idea what she'll say next.

"I knew you wouldn't disappoint me," she says. Wendy looks you up and down; she licks her lips and says, "Will you do what I tell you to?"

You ask, "What do you want me to do?"

She shakes her head, dismissing your question. "Yes or no. It's a simple question, with a simple answer."

• *If you want to know what she's talking about,* PLEASE TURN TO PAGE 89.

• *If you simply say yes,* PLEASE TURN TO PAGE 40.

• *If you say no,* PLEASE TURN TO PAGE 130.

"You're right. We should do something about that." So you're cold, wet, tired. Sarah looks delectable in the candlelight; some fooling around with her should warm you right up. You made this mistake once, taking her for granted, neglecting your sex life. You're not about to do it again. You quickly take off your clothes, then fall onto the bed, covering her body with yours.

She squeals and tries to squirm away. "God, you're freezing!" Her slippery body, sliding beneath yours, is delightful. You grin and grab her wrists, pinning her beneath you.

"I'll have to warm myself up, then, won't I?" You start to rub against her, rotating your hips, rubbing your hardening cock against her heated thighs. It's not long before you're quite hard, and then you push her legs apart with yours, press the tip of your cock against her cunt. It isn't dripping, but it's wet enough to feel good. You slide inside her, not far. "This seems nice and warm. Can I warm myself up here?"

She giggles, then tugs at her wrists. You release her hands, and she laces them around your neck, opening her thighs farther. "Go ahead. I think I can take it." So you slide all the way in, and oh, it's hot in there, hot and wet, slicker than silk against the skin of your cock, and as you start to slide in and out of your lover, you wonder why you even considered just having a cup of soup. It wouldn't have heated you nearly as well as this.

You debate spending Christmas with your parents or Sarah's, but in the end, the two of you decide to spend it alone together in your new apartment. It's your first Christmas in New York, but you don't see much of the city. You stay in bed, for the most part, having sex, reading trashy novels, watching dumb TV. It's a bliss-ful vacation.

When the spring semester starts in January, you create a new tradition; on Fridays Sarah goes to work early so she can leave early, be home to meet you when you get back from teaching. It's a great way to start the weekend, making slow afternoon love with your girlfriend. As January turns to February, you get more and more experimental. You surprise her one day with candles and ice cubes. You visit Toys in Babeland with her and bring home a pair of fur-lined leather cuffs. You cuff Sarah's wrists and then bend her over your knee and spank her lush ass; every yelp makes your cock throb under her until you can't wait any longer—you roll her off you, onto her stomach, and then spread her legs and sink your cock into her cunt, fucking her hard, until she's half falling off the bed.

Afterward, she asks you to do it again.

It's not all about sex. There's romance, too. On February 14, you take Sarah to SoHo, to Savoy. You've been saving up, putting enough money aside that you can afford the four-course prix fixe menu. You take Sarah upstairs to the room holding six small tables. One delicious course follows another, and for the finale, the servers caramelize your crème brûlée over the crackling fire. Sarah is clearly delighted, and you feel happy and cheerfully content as you hold her hand.

Your pleasure is complicated only slightly by an odd coinci-dence—as you're paying for the meal, after Sarah has already headed downstairs to wash her hands and get her coat, Wendy Lake walks into the room.

She sits down at a nearby table, alone, and gazes at the fire. You wonder if she's eating alone on Valentine's Day, or if she's meeting someone. Is Wendy involved in a romance herself? The thought bothers you, though you can't say why. She doesn't seem to have seen you, and you don't see any reason to interrupt her reverie. But as you head downstairs, you keep thinking about Wendy—her pale, perfect face warmed by the shifting firelight.

You see very little of Wendy Lake in the spring semester—she has a break from teaching in order to work on her new book, so she's not in the department much. It's cold enough in February and March that you and Sarah aren't going out much, either; you tend to stay in your apartment, working and talking and having lots of sex. It's a very pleasant way to spend your second semester in New York.

As it gets warmer in late April, you start fooling around outdoors, too, in various parks and open spaces. Your sex life gets better and better—and oddly, that seems to make you more attractive. More of your students are flirting with you; more of your colleagues as well. You're flattered, but you're not about to risk your newfound happiness with Sarah. She's everything a man could ask for in a girlfriend—smart, sweet, awfully pretty, and utterly devoted to you. So you are nothing more than friendly to the various women flirting with you; you're not even tempted. Until, on a Friday afternoon, when you're deep in discussion with one of your brighter students, Wendy Lake walks into your office.

"Hello, Mark." Her voice is low, seductive. The top two buttons of her clingy ice-blue cardigan are unbuttoned, baring more breast than office decorum allows. She's wearing a slim black skirt, slit up the right side to reveal a long, stocking-clad leg. With her hair falling loose down her back, Wendy looks like an invitation to sin.

Your student looks flustered and quickly stands and grabs her books and bag. "Thanks, Professor. See you Monday!" She flashes you a quick smile and ducks out the door.

You frown. "We were still going, Wendy."

She smirks. "You don't want to go too far with that girl, Mark. You could get into trouble." Wendy steps farther into your small office, pushes the door closed with her hip. Suddenly your office feels even smaller.

"Can I help you with something, Professor?" You swivel in your chair to face her. You're not about to try to hide from her.

Wendy says, "Can you help me? Now, that's a good question, Mark. I've noticed the way you run out of here on Friday afternoons, back to that girlfriend of yours."

"Sarah and I are very happy, Wendy. You wouldn't understand." Your voice is calm, even.

"Oh, I'm sure you're *happy*. Everyone in the department knows how happy you are with your little girlfriend." Wendy smiles. It's not a nice smile. "And I think I know *why* you're so happy. I bet I can guess what you've been doing on all those Friday afternoons; what you've been thinking about while you meet with your students." Wendy slips a stocking-clad foot out of her high-heeled shoe; reaching out, she slides it up your leg until it comes to rest in your crotch, against your balls and cock. Your cock hardens. "Oh, yes—I was right, wasn't I? You're ready. I do think you can help me, Mark. I think you can help me quite a bit. And aren't you a bit bored with that sweet girlfriend of yours?"

There's no reason Sarah will ever need to know about it if you give Wendy what she wants. Wendy leans forward, applying more pressure with her foot against your cock. Her cardigan gapes open, exposing more smooth curve of white breast.

- *If you're willing to cheat on Sarah,* PLEASE TURN TO THE NEXT PAGE.

- *If you aren't willing to cheat on Sarah,* PLEASE TURN TO PAGE 196.

Y ou run a hand up Wendy's silky leg, to the edge of her knee-
length skirt. You slide your hand up under her skirt and discover bare thighs and garter straps. Farther up is a thin strip
of fabric, which you easily push aside to reveal her naked pussy, damp
to the touch.

"Now? Here?"

Wendy smiles slowly. "That's up to you, Mark." She tilts her knee
outward, making her cunt more accessible. Your finger dips into her,
strokes in and out a few times. You can smell her arousal, damp and
salty. She presses her cunt up against your finger, makes a small noise
in the back of her throat.

Your cock is throbbing. You want to fuck her right here, bend
her over your desk and shove your cock into her. Dare it all, risk getting caught, getting in trouble with the department, with Sarah. It'd
be such a rush, fucking the famous Wendy Lake right here, where
anyone could walk in.

If you really want to try to juggle two women, discretion might
be the better part of valor.

• *If you keep going in the office,* PLEASE TURN TO PAGE 106.

• *If you take it elsewhere,* PLEASE TURN TO PAGE 220.

"To be honest, I'd rather not." It's not that the idea of her fingers up your ass isn't intriguing, even exciting. But that isn't what you want right now.

"Really?"

"Really." You pull away from her, turn, and look her in the eyes. You take the lube out of her wet hand, drop it on a bookshelf. "What I'd actually enjoy is a blow job. I think you'd enjoy it, too. Why don't you get down on your knees and give me one, Wendy?"

Wendy frowns, but it's not an angry frown. More of a thoughtful one, as if you've surprised her. "You want a blow job? I'll give you one—I'll even give you the best blow job you've ever had. But remember this: I'm not happy with you, Mark."

"I can live with that," you say.

"Can you?" She quirks one arched brow before sliding to her knees, pulling your underwear down, out of the way, and taking your thick cock in her mouth.

You're not sure, to be honest. Wendy's mouth moving on your cock makes it hard to think. She engulfs it at first, sucking gently. It feels incredible, and you harden in her mouth quickly. You bury your hands in her hair—she doesn't seem to mind. She's started licking your cock, twirling her tongue along its length. It's gotten fully hard now; somehow she still has it in her mouth, all the way down to the base. The tip is buried in her throat, and she swallows, the muscles of her throat massaging it.

You've never felt anything like this—Sarah gave blow jobs, but not like this. Hers involved a lot of sliding back and forth, her whole body moving up and down. Wendy, by contrast, is barely moving—her tongue and throat are doing all the work, but God, they do good work. Her hands are pressed against your bare thighs, her nails are

digging into your skin. Maybe it hurts—you can't tell. All your attention is focused on the intense pleasure in your cock, on the pressure
building in your groin. Your fingers tug at her hair, and you half
expect her to complain, but instead she moans softly.

So you tug harder, pull Wendy even deeper onto your cock. You
look down at her wet lips moving hungrily against your skin. It all
feels good, so good, and your hips start to move in time with the
motion of her mouth, her throat. You're fucking her face, and she's
whimpering, she's taking it all deep, and the pure sensation of it feels
better than anything has ever felt before. You fuck harder, fuck her
open mouth, and it's coming, you're coming, you're coming hard.
Your hands clench in her hair, shoving her up against your cock, her
face pressed against your groin, your cock deep in her throat. And
you come like that, long spurts down her swallowing, pulsing throat;
you come until you're exhausted, and only then do you let her go.
You're shaking.

• PLEASE TURN TO PAGE 165.

"Not here, Wendy. Not now." You place a hand gently on her shoulder again, but she shrugs it off, violently this time, and spins around to face you.

"Coward." She spits the word at you. She's angry—angrier than she has any reason to be. Maybe that marriage comment hit a nerve.

"Wendy, there are plenty of things I'd love to do with you. But not here. Let me take you somewhere else, please."

"Forget it. It's over, Mark." She's stalking off down the stone hallway, her red skirt flaring around her legs.

You follow her out to the parking lot, hoping to talk some sense into her, but she climbs into a red BMW and roars away, leaving you standing there. You're bewildered, frustrated, and upset. But you can't do a damn thing about it.

As you start walking back to the subway, you try to tell yourself that it's all for the best. Things had gotten so strange, so quickly. Wendy Lake was fascinating and a lot of fun, but there was something unbalanced, obsessive, about her. She pulled you along in her wake, but now you've come to your senses. You tell yourself that you'll meet somebody else—someone with whom you can have a healthy, normal relationship. A relationship of equals. You tell yourself that you'll be fine.

Somehow you're just not convinced.

THE END

This isn't your scene. Naked strangers: You expected to be aroused, but the whole thing turns you off instead of on. It feels strange, artificial—beautiful people, waxed and oiled and burnished until they shine, moving around like choreographed figures in a dance, a dream of sexuality unrestrained. It's sensual, perhaps, but not sexy. They're all trying too hard. You stand there for a minute, watching them. There's a tap on your shoulder. You turn to see Wendy Lake walking toward you, wearing a see-through slip that she's reaching down to smooth against her thighs. You wonder if she was fucking someone else with that slip pushed up around her waist, and the thought makes you feel sick. You don't want to be where some other man just was. It's not a bad fantasy, but it doesn't work in real life.

"You're still wearing clothes, Mark." She arches an eyebrow, shakes her head slightly, as if you've been a naughty boy. The gesture makes you feel contrary; you don't feel like indulging her whims. And you're angry, too. You don't know why she felt the need to do this, to have this sex party, to fuck other men in public, right in front of you. What does that say about you? Aren't you enough for her?

You shrug. "I don't think I'll be staying." Your tone is harsh, dismissive. You want to hurt Wendy, want her to know that you're not impressed with this decadent orgy of shifting flesh.

"I'm disappointed." Her voice is flat, calm, as if she's discussing the weather. "I didn't expect you to have a problem with this."

"And if I do have a problem with it? What then, Wendy?" You want her to say that she'll leave this party, that she doesn't really care about it, that she wants only you.

Wendy shrugs. "Then you should either go home and sulk, or stay and get over it. Whatever makes you happy." She turns away, heading back into the crowd.

You want to reach out, to grab Wendy's shoulder and pull her back. You want to fuck her, up against a wall or on the cold slate floor of this hallway. You want to show her that she's yours, that she belongs with you, belongs to you. But she doesn't.

So you turn and walk back to the elevator. You take it down, not bothering to nod at the doorman this time. You're not planning on coming back here—whatever your future in New York holds, it won't be holding any more of Wendy Lake. You can live with that.

THE END

You don't see Wendy Lake over the next few days. You leave a note in her box, asking to see her again, but there's no response. You're having trouble concentrating on your work; the lines of medieval Latin blur across the computer screen, turning into unreadable gibberish. You sit in your office with the door open, hoping she'll walk by. Nothing. You're fascinated by her, but repelled, too. You can't figure out what it is about her. Maybe you should have let her stick her fingers up your ass—maybe she's annoyed enough that she's going to drop you entirely. You leave her another note, asking if you've done something wrong.

It's not until Friday evening, at the end of the first week of classes, when you've settled down to immerse yourself in work, determined to start making a good impression on the new department, that your phone rings.

"I'm naked, Mark. I'm lying naked on my bed, with three fingers in my pussy. Do you want to see me naked, Mark? I want to see you naked. . . ."

"Hello, Wendy." Your voice trembles slightly, betraying your excitement. You take a quick breath, trying to steady yourself.

"I think everyone should see you naked. I bet you have a beautiful body. I want women to look at you and wonder what your naked body looks like."

"And how will you accomplish that?" You're intrigued, titillated by the notion of women everywhere looking at your naked body, desiring it.

Wendy's voice grows sharp, commanding. "Take off all your clothes, put on a coat and sneakers, and come over. Take the subway, not a cab. I'll know if you cheat."

You have a wool coat that'll come down almost to your ankles.

What she's suggesting is illegal—and more to the point, she's back to giving you orders again. If you let her get away with that, you don't know where she'll take you next.

- *If you do what she tells you to*, PLEASE TURN TO PAGE 42.

- *If you say no*, PLEASE TURN TO PAGE 202.

Wendy doesn't call you Tuesday night. Or Wednesday. You tell yourself it doesn't matter. You've known the woman for only two days—how can it possibly matter whether she calls you or not?

It matters.

You occupy yourself with classes, orientation meetings, lunches with colleagues. It's the start of the semester—your first semester as an adjunct professor. This is what you spent six years of graduate school working toward; it should be exciting, invigorating. Instead, it's annoying. You're not thinking about the ancient Greeks or Romans; you're not interested in engaging young freshman minds. The life of the mind doesn't compare to the life of the body. You can't stop thinking about Wendy Lake's tight cunt, about her breasts in your hands, even about the smears of dirt left on her red dress. And when you're not thinking about Wendy, you're thinking about women—their soft skin, the way they smell. There are women everywhere on this campus.

At Thursday's lecture, you fixate on the speaker, Belinda Lundstrom. She's an attractive brunette: shoulder-length, wavy hair, hazel-green eyes. Not spectacular like Wendy, but quite pretty, and with a nice, curvy body. Big handfuls of breasts. Her voice is sexy, too; low and hoarse. You can imagine her moaning underneath you. You can imagine Wendy naked there, too—though you're not sure what she'd be doing. Sucking a nipple on one of Belinda's large breasts? You wonder what Belinda's nipples look like. You wonder what her pussy hair looks like, feels like. You don't hear a word of the lecture.

During the Q&A session afterward, you feel the pressure of Benjamin's regard; he keeps glancing over at you, expecting you to say something. Normally, you would have—Belinda's work is related to some of the themes in your own dissertation—but you keep your mouth shut and your head down, and as soon as the group starts breaking up, you slip discreetly out the door.

When you come home, there's no message on your machine. You should work, but you can't concentrate. You sit by the phone, your hand inside your sweats, stroking your dick, willing the phone to ring. Eight. Eight-thirty. Nine. Ten. At eleven, you go to bed; there's a lecture in the morning you need to attend. At midnight, the phone rings. You're still awake.

• PLEASE TURN TO PAGE 81.

It isn't worth the risk. Now you have to keep from admitting that you're backing down. "You know, Wendy, the more I think about it, the more I think I might like to lick you tonight after all. Spread you out on the bed with your legs up in the air, lick your pussy, your clit, until you're whimpering, begging for it—and if you're very good, maybe I'll let you come." You try to sound intense, dominant, powerful.

"Just come over, Mark." Wendy chuckles and hangs up the phone. You know then that you'll never get her to do what you want. Wendy Lake will always be the one calling the shots. As you head over to her apartment on the subway, as you suck her pussy and then head home again in the early morning—*without* the promised blow job—you can't stop thinking about that fact.

She's a gorgeous woman; you try to tell yourself that you don't mind being at her beck and call. You see her every few nights (and try not to think about whom she might be with on the other nights). Some weeks she refuses to see you at all. And then, in early November, she starts bringing other women into bed with you. There's a Japanese girl, Yumiko, who comes over pretty often, and a redhead, Maggie. You think Maggie is in love with Wendy, but you're not sure.

It's fun, fucking them, but what you want is Wendy. Wendy's there, but she's accessible to you only when she wants to be, when it suits her, when it serves her power games. She never lets you choose the sexual activity; she never comes over to your place; she never lets you stay the night. You wish that just once, she would be more agreeable—do something for you, something to make you happy. But it never happens. Not once.

It's all driving you crazy. Maybe that's what leads you into trouble.

• PLEASE TURN TO PAGE 212.

Y ou're curious but also cautious. "I might be. It depends. What does fooling around entail?"

Rick smiles. He's got great teeth, too. "Whatever you like. We could fuck, or I could suck your cock, or you could suck mine. If you haven't been with a guy before, maybe I should just suck your cock. I'd enjoy that."

How bad can that be? It's like having a woman suck it, right? Especially if you close your eyes. It'll be an adventure. You probably won't even get hard—or if you do, you're not likely to come, given that you've emptied your balls into his wife's cunt.

"Okay." Your heart is thumping harder—or maybe you're noticing it only now.

The three of you walk over to an unoccupied corner, over by the tall bookshelf and the wide windows, away from the bar. You lean back against an exposed brick wall. Rick kneels in front of you. You close your eyes. The whiskey is working on you, making you feel nice and relaxed. This is going to be fine. It'll be like when Wendy goes down on you, or when Sarah used to—though that was a long time ago.

And then Rick's mouth is on your limp cock, the cock still glistening, covered in his wife's wetness, and it's nothing like Wendy's or Sarah's mouths at all. You can't describe the difference—can't even pinpoint what it is. He seems to know exactly how hard to suck, where the tender bits are, where his tongue will feel the best, caressing the skin. You harden quickly in his agile mouth. He takes the length of your cock eagerly, making small sounds of pleasure as he hungrily eats you. You ought to be bothered, disturbed—this is a man sucking your cock. But you can't worry about that, not when this feels so good. Who cares who or what it is? As long as it feels this good. His finger is pressing gently into your ass, his other hand is coming up to cup your balls, to caress them, until you can't help it, you do what you'd never have anticipated you might, you come explosively in another man's mouth.

Rick pulls away, slurping gently, dropping a quick kiss on your cock as he goes. The kiss does bother you, but it would feel ungracious to complain about it after all his hard work. He kneels at your feet, looking up at you.

"So, what did you think?"

It felt great—but the question you have to face now is, are you a man who lets other men suck your cock, stick their fingers in your ass? You can't pretend you're experimenting if you keep going with this—you liked it too much. Would you consider sucking some other guy's cock? Would you consider doing more? Or does the whole experience make your stomach churn, make you wish you hadn't gone there at all? You've learned something about what turns you on; the question is, do you want to learn more?

- *If you liked it and want more,* PLEASE TURN TO PAGE 36.

- *If the whole thing makes you queasy and you want to pretend it never happened,* PLEASE TURN TO PAGE 67.

You almost lean forward. Almost pull Ruth into a kiss; you know she'd be eager. Your cock is throbbing in your pants—you have to stand up, walk behind the desk, and cut office hours short, sending Ruth away. She looks disappointed, hurt, as she leaves your small office; she doesn't understand how bad it could have been. Of course she doesn't. It's your job to understand that when they can't. That's the point.

After she leaves, you sit down at your desk, shaken. You'd never thought you were the kind of man to take advantage of one of your students, someone who looks up to you as an authority figure. And to make it worse, Ruth is underage! What are you turning into? What is New York doing to you?

Maybe it's not New York. Maybe it's Wendy Lake. With all her sexual escapades, somehow your body has started to feel entitled to sex, whenever and wherever it wants it. If this goes on, maybe the next student you're tempted by won't even be willing or eager. Maybe the next time, you won't hold back.

You pick up the phone and call Wendy. She isn't there, so you end up leaving a message on her machine.

"Wendy, it's been great. But I think I need to call this off; things are getting crazy on my end. I need to concentrate on work for a while. Best of luck to you. I hope we can stay friends."

After you put the phone down, you rest your head on your desk. You're incredibly aroused; your head is pounding with frustrated desire. But you've been frustrated before, you can live with that. You couldn't have lived with yourself if you'd acted any differently.

• PLEASE TURN TO PAGE 85.

You hesitate, tempted. You could go there, you could do more with Rick. He's looking at you with big puppy-dog eyes; his expression is oddly intent. It's as if he wants something from you—something more than sex. It makes you uncomfortable, and honestly, you'd rather spend the time with Wendy, if you can. You try to let Rick down gently. "I appreciate the offer, but I'm afraid I have another commitment tomorrow night. Maybe another time . . ." You trail off gently.

"Sure, sure." He looks disappointed but not upset. "Well, see you around." And then Rick is taking Rhonda's hand and leading her away, leaving you to wander back across the room, to where Wendy is pressed up against a marble pillar, getting a very thorough fucking. You pause several feet away, just watching.

➤

Wendy's partner seems like he's getting close—he's pounding faster and faster. It's strange, watching another man's ass move that fast. Finally, he finishes. He pulls out then, and you catch a glimpse of his face as he turns: fine-boned and oddly serene. He walks away without a word to Wendy. She catches her breath, pulls her chemise back down to her thighs, and then walks over to you, passing various people tangled in couples and larger groups on the floor.

She steps up close to you and tilts an eyebrow. "So, Rick didn't work out for you? I thought you might like him."

"I tried it, but I don't think guys are my thing." You don't feel like explaining to Wendy that you'd enjoyed it, but you still didn't want to do it again. You're happier with her assuming you didn't enjoy it.

She smiles. "I hope it was at least interesting."

"Definitely." You hesitate, not sure how to phrase your desire. She doesn't say anything helpful—just stands there, looking at you. You're reminded once again that you're naked and she isn't. Does this amuse her? Does she feel more powerful, dressed among the naked?

"So . . . would you like to have sex with me?" You can't quite bring yourself to ask if she wants to fuck. This is vaguer, more open to interpretation. Though actually, you'd be perfectly happy fucking, sliding your cock into her warm cunt. Even if it is dripping with another man's come at the moment. Maybe *because* it is. The thought of it is starting to make you hard again.

She tilts her head, considering. "I wouldn't mind being finger-fucked. I didn't actually come with Christian. He's single-minded with his fucking; it's all about him. Do you think you can make me come?"

It wasn't what you'd had in mind, but you can't back down from a challenge like that. "I can try."

"Try hard." And she's sitting on the floor, lying down, spreading her legs wide, her knees slightly bent. You lie beside her, your hand reaching between her thighs. Your body is pressed against hers, and you realize that this is the most body contact you've had with her so far. Your cock throbs and grows hard against her thigh. But you're going to have to ignore it for now.

You slide your fingers into her cunt; it's loose, sopping, with a mix of her fluids and Christian's. And maybe other men's—you don't know how many men she fucked before you arrived. You can fit two fingers in easily, even three. You finger-fuck her simply for a while, sliding in and out. She seems to enjoy it; her breathing gets faster, and she arches her hips to meet you. But she doesn't seem to be getting close to coming. You add your thumb on her clit, dipping it into her cunt to wet it, then rubbing in slow circles, dipping again whenever it gets too dry. That helps; she's making tiny moans, encouraging you. You bend over and take one of her chemise-covered breasts in your mouth; the fabric is thin enough that you can feel the slight ridges in her aureole. You lick and suck and nibble, and finally you bite, and that's when she arches up to you, that's when she whispers, "Fist-fuck me, Mark, if you can. I want your whole fist in my cunt."

You have no idea how to do that. You slide another finger in—four is easy enough. You slide in and out, and she's tight around you, but not too tight. You can do that. But when you try to add your thumb, it doesn't get very far. You can bury your fingers and thumb, but there's no way you're getting your knuckles into her cunt, even as wet and dripping as it is. Maybe your hand is too big. You move faster, fucking with your fingers, practically chewing on her nipple, and at last her pussy clenches around your fingers, squeezing them like a tight fist, and she's coming, arching upward with a small scream. You managed to get her off, but you feel nonetheless like you didn't quite measure up.

You pull your hand out, and Wendy says, "Thanks."

"You're welcome."

"I should go check on my other guests. Have a good time." And she's getting up and walking away, leaving you with a hard-on and nowhere to put it.

You get up, too, and wander around, but everyone seems pretty well occupied. You watch for a while, but it gets to be too much. You're starting to feel horny again, but you don't want to be the guy masturbating alone in a corner at a sex party. So you go back to the small guest bedroom, find your pile of clothes, and pull them on. It's surreal, getting dressed while hearing the sounds of ardent sex going on in the background. You take the elevator down, nod to the doorman, and go home to jerk off in peace.

It's been a very strange night.

• PLEASE TURN TO PAGE 38.

Of course you're going to call her. You're too intrigued not to. You work hard all the next day; it's a good distraction from thoughts of Wendy Lake. Though it's impossible to stop thinking about her entirely. When you call that night, Wendy's voice sounds entirely ordinary. You're relieved—two nights in a row would have been a bit much. She invites you over. You're tempted to take a cab, but that would be expensive and might seem desperate. You take the subway and get to her place in less than twenty minutes.

Wendy lives on Riverside Drive—a nice part of town, not grand, but with pleasant, tree-lined streets and lovely old buildings. Much, much nicer than where you live. Her building is perhaps a bit older than some of the others on the street, slightly more faded. A wrinkled old man in uniform takes your name, giving you a brief up-and-down examination when you say you're here to see Wendy Lake. He doesn't seem impressed, but he sends you up in the elevator to the penthouse floor. When the door opens, you understand why the grouchy doorman didn't think you were up to her standards.

You walk into a magnificent apartment. It's huge. Endless windows open on to a wide terrace. All of it done up with mid-century modern furniture and plush leather couches. Fine Persian rugs cover the floors, and an erotic painting that looks like it was done by Matisse hangs on the wall. A Roman statue of Pan—lewd, ecstatic, driving his cock into a goat—takes pride of place in the living room.

"Nice place." It's a vast understatement, but you don't know what else to say. Her books must sell very well, indeed. Your entire apartment would fit into her living room. You feel like you've shrunk an inch or two.

"Can I get you a drink? Dinner?" She gives you a long, thoughtful look. What is going on behind those beautiful eyes?

"A drink would be great." Anything to steady your nerves; being around this woman throws you off balance.

"Coming right up." She goes to the kitchen, leaving you alone.

You drift over to a tall bookshelf in the far corner. Books are reassuring. Several copies of each of her books take up one long shelf—it's impressive, in a way, but also somewhat off-putting. It's like bragging, having your books out like that. Slightly tacky. Wendy does have plenty of other good books, including a rare edition of Sappho's love poems, the ancient Greek side by side with the English translations. You page through and find an old favorite: "Without warning / as a whirlwind / swoops on an oak / Love shakes my heart."

"Ah, Sappho. *You appear as a god to me,*" Wendy says as she walks back into the room and hands you a glass of wine.

You contemplate quoting the next line of the famous poem back to her, but for some reason you are too shy. You take a sip of the wine. It's incredibly good. What a difference from the ten-dollar-a-bottle stuff you can barely afford to buy.

"Beautiful wine." You hold up your glass to her. "Beautiful books. Beautiful woman."

Wendy takes the book from you and flips through it, her hands gentle on the pages. She pauses to read a few lines. You imagine yourself on ancient Lesbos, sea and sun caressing you as you listen to your lover sing antique love songs under an impossibly blue sky. Wendy runs a finger along one line and says quietly, "I used to have ideas about Sappho. There's this bit, in one of the poems—well, it's intriguing. It might mean . . . something." She raises an eyebrow, glances at you. "When I was in graduate school, I planned on writing a monograph about it."

"Why didn't you?" You're curious. You might enjoy reading that monograph. Wendy's other books don't appeal to you.

She chuckles. "Oh, I don't know." She smiles, a little sadly, and puts the book carefully back on the shelf. "My other work is much more profitable."

"But still . . ."

"Mark, did you really come here to talk about Sappho?" She smiles.

You flush. "No."

"Good. Come on, then." And she walks away, out of the living room and into the bedroom. You follow her.

She pulls her dress off in a single, smooth motion—she's naked underneath it. You start removing your own clothes, impatient with the layers and buttons. Wendy sits down on the bed, cross-legged, waiting for you. She's lit only by the ambient city lights coming through the window; it's enough. She's gorgeous, and your cock practically jumps out of your pants when you unzip them.

When you're finally naked, she asks solemnly, "So, which will it be—anal, oral, or regular old intercourse?"

You don't want to pick. "We can't have all three?"

Wendy grins. "Good answer." And then she's reaching for you, pulling you onto the bed, falling back against the pillows. Her hands are on your head, urging you down, and you go willingly, diving for her pussy, spreading her legs apart with your hands, your tongue landing unerringly on her clit. She shivers when you lick her, and her fingers curl in your hair. The scent of her cunt hardens your cock; you're longing to drive yourself deep inside her. But you want her to be hungry for you, begging for you, by then. So you take it slow at first, licking and sucking, nibbling the flesh of her outer lips.

You tease her with light flicks of your tongue, with a finger dipping into her now-wet cunt, then slipping out again, until she's pressing her cunt against your mouth, your hand. Until she's whimpering, twisting in the sheets, her fingers pressing against your skull as if she could drive right through the bone. That's when you slide a finger in, curving it up to find that sweet spot. When you press against her in the right way, with your wet mouth on her hard clit, when you rub the soft flesh, Wendy arches almost off the bed; she gasps for breath and then comes, screaming.

It's a good beginning.

You're drowsy and fall asleep on the dimly lit bed; you've had hours of energetic sex and you've come twice—once in Wendy's mouth, once in her pussy. Maybe all three was a bit ambitious for one night. She's curled in the crook of your arm, her head resting against your shoulder. It's nice; it reminds you of all those nights with Sarah. But in a good way—the thought doesn't sting the way it would have this summer. You're starting to drift off into dreams when Wendy shakes your arm, waking you up.

"What?" You're startled, shaken from sleep.

"Mark. You need to go." She sounds sleepy, too, but firm.

"I thought I could crash here . . . It's late, Wendy." You bend to kiss her cheek, but she pulls away, sitting up.

"Sorry—firm policy. No sleeping over. One of my rules."

You groan but get up and start dressing. "Wish you'd told me before. Are there more rules I should know about?"

"Probably." She doesn't say anything else, simply watches until you're ready to go.

"Good night, Wendy."

You're walking out the door when she says quietly, "Call me tomorrow, Mark."

"Okay."

You spend the next nine nights at Wendy's. Usually, you have dinner together first; she orders incredible food to be delivered from restaurants you could never afford. You feed each other tidbits; you eat off each others' bodies. Inevitably, you move to the bedroom, and the sex gets more focused, more intense. Every night it gets better. But it's not just the sex that keeps you coming back, it's her. The sound of Wendy's voice, her sarcastic quips, her rare smiles. You find yourself thinking about her while you teach, while you're trying to study. You go to her eagerly, you fuck gloriously, and then she sends you home. That part is awkward, uncomfortable, but it seems a small price to pay for this kind of satisfaction. You can't get enough of her. Night after night after night, for nine nights in a row—then, on the tenth day, she doesn't call.

You wait by the phone. You try her at the office. Wendy isn't answering there or at home. You convince yourself that there's a good reason for her not calling, and then five minutes later, you convince yourself that she's dropping you, she's lost interest, she never wants to see you, never wants to fuck you again. You go to bed exhausted, even though you've gotten nothing done.

The next night the phone rings at nine.

"Hello?"

"Mark. Want to come over?" Wendy says as if nothing's happened. You want to ask her what she was doing last night, why she didn't call. Where she was, who she was with. But you're not ready to push her on this. Maybe it was a onetime thing—maybe she had theater tickets with an old friend or went to visit her parents. There are all kinds of simple explanations. So you don't ask. You say, "Sure— I'll be there soon."

As the weeks pass, you find yourself spending most nights at Wendy's apartment. You enjoy her company more and more, and she seems happier when she's with you. But no matter how good your conversations are, how good the sex is, every night she sends you home. As the nights get colder, as September turns to October, that gets harder and harder to take. Part of it is simply annoying, a frustrating inconvenience. It's no fun, taking the subway home in the cold, the late nights, the early mornings. But more than that, you want to know Wendy better. You know her physically, mentally, but there's a big emotional wall between you. Or not a wall—a sheet of one-way glass. You don't see her, but she sees you.

"Mark . . ." She's sleepy, satiated, after a long bout of sex. Tonight you learned about fist fucking; you're still amazed that you could get your whole fist inside her.

"Yes, Wendy?"

"Tell me a story." She asks this often.

"What kind of story would you like tonight?"

Wendy thinks for a moment. "Tell me about your brother."

"Jules? Now, why would you want to hear about a loser like Jules when you have a great guy like me right here?" You stroke Wendy's hair, tangled and damp.

She chuckles. "Just tell me. I want to know."

So you tell her about Jules, the big brother who used to lock you in the basement, who sat on you when he wanted the TV remote, who would twist your arm up behind your back and threaten to break it if you didn't give him your comic books. Jules, who ended up as a lawyer, and a good one. An idealistic, hardworking lawyer, fiercely committed to the idea of justice; he'll probably be a judge someday.

You tell her story after story about Jules that night. Other nights you tell her about your parents, about your friends in grad school, about Sarah—the good parts and the very bad. But when you ask her about herself, the answer is always the same.

You say, "Your turn now. Tell me a story."

Wendy shrugs. "I can't tell stories, Mark. You know that. Besides, I'm horny. I'm going to suck your cock, if you don't object."

"How can I object to that?"

You can't, but as Wendy rolls over on top of you, as she starts kissing her way down your body, you wish for something more. She keeps everything locked away—all the passion, the intensity. You could try to push, but she clearly wants her space. Are you willing to risk it? Even if you manage to unlock her emotions, they might not be pleasant ones.

It's very late again, and you're both naked, lying flat on the bed after a long night of sex. Wendy says, "I'm exhausted. I need to get some sleep." That's your cue to get up and go.

Your stomach feels tight. But you're not willing to keep being some kind of sex toy for Wendy. You want more from her.

You roll over, looking down at her. "Wendy, I'd like to stay." With one hand you start stroking her hair, while the other comes to rest on her bare stomach.

She blinks up at you. "You know the rules, Mark."

"Are the rules really that important?" You try to keep the tone light, but you also keep your eyes locked on hers. The small bedside lamp casts cold shadows across her face. Wendy pulls away from your hands, sits up.

"Yes, yes, they are. Don't cross me, Mark." Her voice is cold, harsh.

What's happening? You thought you were friends, at least, and you're suddenly back to this? "Or else what?"

"Or else that's it. It's over." Her eyes are completely empty. You can't read them at all; it's as if she has no emotions, as if she doesn't care about you at all, one way or the other.

"Just like that?" And it hurts; you hadn't expected it to hurt. Somehow, in the last few weeks, Wendy has gotten under your skin. You've started caring for her, and the idea that she can walk away from you, from this, without a backward glance or a twinge, sends a sharp pain through your belly. You realize that she's never going to let you get closer to her than you are now—and that's not good enough for you.

You say, "Fine, then. I'll go." If she wants to be cold, you can be cold, too. There's no expression in your face—or at least you hope there isn't—as you pull away from her, ready to climb out of bed. And maybe Wendy never thought you'd go, never thought you would leave her, because she's suddenly, unexpectedly, hitting you. These aren't girly slaps—she's pounding your arms and your chest with her fists as hard she can. Wendy is hitting you and saying, over and over, "What the hell do you want from me?"

You barely feel the first couple of punches, but it isn't long before they start to actually hurt. "Hey—hey!" You try to grab her wrists, but she's moving too fast, pounding into you; you can't catch hold. So you give up on that—instead, you move over her, quickly, using your weight and size to pin Wendy to the bed, pushing her arms underneath your chest, wrapping your arms around her to hold her still. But that doesn't work, either, because instead of keeping still, she's licking you, biting your shoulder, your neck, writhing her naked body underneath yours. Wendy is whispering, begging, "Mark, fuck me. Please. Mark, I need you. I need you to fuck me, hard. Hard and fast. Please, Mark. Please . . ." And she's opening her legs, sliding her wet pussy up against your cock, and you can't help getting hard, with her voice in your ear, her hands sliding out to circle you, to dig nails into your back, to push your ass where she wants it to go.

• *If you go with it and slide in,* PLEASE TURN TO PAGE 93.

• *If you resist her and pull away,* PLEASE TURN TO PAGE 69.

Y ou look at her again, and she meets your gaze steadily. Her face is flushed; her lips look soft, bruised. Maybe this isn't wise, but you would really like to kiss her.

"I'd love to go to your place."

Belinda drains her coffee in a quick gulp, then stands up. You leave yours behind. It's a few blocks to her building, one of the university-owned apartment buildings on 112th Street—it's much nicer than your place. It's clean, for one thing, and has its own antique charm. As you ride up the elevator, you realize that this is the sort of place you might end up living in, if the university decides to keep you. But you can't think about that now—you need to concentrate on Belinda. It's not long before you're inside her apartment, standing in her living room, not sure what to do next. She solves that puzzle for you by stepping forward and kissing you. Her hands slide around to the small of your back, and her mouth is moving eagerly on yours. You kiss her back; she tastes like coffee with a hint of mint. It's a good taste. And she smells divine to you; sweat and a delicate, powdery scent.

She's pressed up close against you, her breasts against your chest, her hips against yours. She's almost your height. Your cock quickly grows hard, and you ease her over to the couch. The gray dress has buttons all down the front; you start unbuttoning them, exposing soft, full breasts in a satiny black bra. It has a front clasp.

You keep kissing her while you undo the clasp, and then her breasts are free from the bra, heavy in your cupped hands. Your cock pulses against your pants, and your heart is thumping. You rub your thumbs over the nipples; they get hard, and Belinda makes a small sound in the back of her throat. You bend down, press her back against the arm of the couch, and take one nipple into your mouth, licking and sucking, while you knead the other breast with your hand. She whimpers louder and arches up toward you. You switch breasts, then go back. The right seems a little more sensitive than the left one—she moans louder when you suckle that one. Your balls are starting to ache, and you reach to unbutton more of her dress. That's when she stops you.

She reaches down, catches your hand in hers.

"Mark, I want to suck you." Belinda looks at you with eyes very wide, almost pleading. You've never had a woman actively *want* to go down on you before. What can you do but acquiesce? You lean back against the sofa. She undoes your pants, and you help her remove them. Then she slides down to kneel between your legs, her breasts pressed up between your thighs, against your balls. She bends forward, kisses the tip of your erect cock. Then she licks it, gently, almost delicately. Belinda licks all around it, and the slow pace is driving you crazy . . . but you're not about to interrupt.

Eventually, she leans forward, pressing her breasts harder against your heavy balls, and takes your cock entirely into her mouth. She moans then, a pleased, satisfied sound. Then she starts to lick, to suck, to move up and down the length of your cock. She puts her whole body into it, sliding up and down, her large breasts surrounding your cock, the soft flesh of them enveloping you. She's whimpering and moaning and even talking around your cock—you can't make out what she's saying, but just the motion of her mouth is enough to make your balls tighten, make the jism rise. Your pulse starts racing and you lean forward, you tangle your fingers in her soft brown curls as her mouth moves faster, faster, until you're coming, coming in her wet mouth, and she swallows it hungrily. When you're finished, she licks you clean, then sits back on her heels, smiling.

"Good?" Belinda seems anxious, and you hurry to reassure her, reaching out a hand to take hers. Her slim fingers interlace with yours.

"Really good." And it was—it was an excellent blow job. You feel sleepy and warm; your eyelids want to close. You let them, for one splendid moment. You want to lie back and nap; you feel so relaxed and satisfied. But that would be rude. You force your eyes open again, smile at Belinda, tug at her hand. "Can I do something for you?"

"No, I'm okay." She's smiling and climbing up on the couch next to you, curling into your arm. That's fine; you can always do something for her later. When you've had the chance to rest a bit. You close your eyes again.

You wake to find her shaking your arm gently. "Mark—Mark, wake up."

"Sorry about that." You hadn't meant to fall asleep, she had simply sucked all the stress and tension out of you. It seemed like the first time you'd felt content since last spring, when you walked in on Sarah and that guy.

Belinda smiles. "It's okay, but I need to go. There's a history seminar I promised to attend. 'Medieval Saints: Epileptics or Holy Women?' I'm sorry to kick you out."

"No, that's okay." You're still sleepy, dazed. But you can think clearly enough to know that you want to see more of her, do more with her. "Can I call you tomorrow?" You're standing up, pulling your clothes together.

"I'd like that." She ushers you out the door, still smiling.

You whistle as you walk home. It's a perfect late afternoon on a beautiful fall day—too nice to take the subway. You can't wait to see Belinda Lundstrom again.

The next week is busy, but you manage to have lunch with Belinda a few times. You attend lectures together; you spend time in her office, talking over your work. She seems oddly sad at times—you set yourself a challenge to make her laugh, as often as possible. You tell bad Latin jokes—*How do you know third and fourth conjugation verbs will never be married? They have no "bo"s in their future.* That one went over surprisingly well, but not as well as the classic *No Latin student can decline sex.* You're amazed she'd never heard that one before, but also delighted to be the one to tell it to her.

When you run out of jokes, you start translating silly phrases into Latin. *Estne ariena in toga, an solum tibi libet me videre?* Is that a banana in your toga, or are you just happy to see me? Or, *Quantum materiae materietur marmota monax si marmota monax materiam possit materiari?* She has a wonderful laugh, rich and full. By the end of the week, the assistants have started smiling at you—Belinda seems to be a general favorite in the department, and they're happy to see her happy. You're happy, too; you've never been involved with someone who appreciates your work before. You didn't know what you were missing.

On Friday night, you take her out to dinner. It's silly—she probably makes two or three times as much as you do. Still, you want to be the one to treat. You have Thai food and discover that you both love the green curry chicken. And when you go back to her place, Belinda doesn't even ask what you want—she takes you to her bed, undoes your pants, and takes your cock in her eager mouth. You've been wanting her all night; in the restaurant, your eyes had kept dropping to the top button on her black dress, itching to unbutton it and reveal those generous breasts. Your fingers slide into her soft hair; your hips arch up to meet her mouth, and it's not long before you're coming, deep in her throat.

Belinda slides up into your arms again afterward. But you're not sleepy this time. You reach down, start unbuttoning her dress. You want to see her naked. You want to touch her bare skin, all over; you want to find her pussy and give her an orgasm. And once you've recovered a bit, you'd really like to make love to her. But she tenses at your touch, and then reaches out to stop your hand. She's biting her lip, pulling away.

"What's wrong?" You're bewildered. She's willing to give you blow jobs but won't let you do anything else?

Belinda curls up on the bed next to you. She says, "Mark, I like you. I like you a lot. But I can't fuck you."

You're startled: first by her direct language, second by what she's just said. "Umm . . . why not?" You don't want to be pushy, but she seems to like you fine, and it's not as if she's a virgin—she was married!

Belinda says softly, slowly, "It—it was the accident. I was in the car, too. Joseph died. I just got hurt. Pretty badly. My pelvis shattered; they didn't think I'd be able to walk again. I can walk fine, but I can't have intercourse. It hurts too much. I'm sorry."

That's a lot to take in. Before you can, she goes on, quicker, urgent.

"It doesn't mean we can't do stuff. I really like going down on you—I can do that as much as you want, as often as you want. And you can go down on me, if you want to, if you're careful." Her voice drops. "I think we might even be able to do anal stuff. If you want. But no intercourse."

Really no intercourse? Ever? "You've tried—"

"Yes!" Belinda says it sharply, almost angrily. Then her voice softens again. "You'll have to trust me, Mark. The guy was gentle, and pretty damn small, physically. A lot smaller than you. It was unbearable."

Well, that's clear enough. But what do you want to do about it? You really like Belinda; you could keep seeing her, despite the restriction. You can't even begin to take in what that would mean—if you started seeing her seriously, exclusively, that would mean never having normal sex for the rest of your life. Could you do that? Would it drive you crazy? And maybe it's nuts to think about it, but what if things got serious? You'd been expecting to marry Sarah, to have children with her someday. Could Belinda even have children? It's a lot to think about, to take in.

"Belinda, I'll need to think about this. Look, I'll call you tomorrow, okay?" You hate to come and run, but you can't make a decision right now. You pull up your pants and stand up. She's standing up, too, buttoning her dress.

"Sure, I understand." Her voice is bleak, empty. She's not expecting you to call. "I'll talk to you tomorrow, then." She looks up at you, managing a smile. "Whatever you decide, I've enjoyed this week."

"Me, too." And then she's opening the door, and you're stepping through, and she's closing it behind you.

You walk home slowly. When you get back, you end up wandering aimlessly around your apartment, thinking. You can't concentrate on work; you're too busy trying to imagine what your life would be like with Belinda. All the blow jobs you want, all the time. Sarah hadn't liked giving you blow jobs; she'd do it, but you always felt like she wanted to be doing something else. Anything else. There was a lot to be said for eager blow jobs. But no normal sex? At all?

Belinda shares your academic interests, your approach to life and work. You can imagine falling in love with her. You can imagine a future with her, but it would come at a price. It would take energy, effort. Time and attention and an emotional risk. And you honestly don't know if you could handle it—never actually fucking again.

You don't sleep well. In the morning, you decide you'd better call Belinda right away. No point in dragging this out. The only thing is, you're still not sure what you're going to say. You reach for the phone anyway; maybe you'll figure it out when you hear that soft, sexy voice. You dial Belinda's number.

• *If you say yes to Belinda,* PLEASE TURN TO PAGE 61.

• *If you say no to Belinda,* PLEASE TURN TO PAGE 65.

"Wendy, I can't. Ask me for something else." It's too dangerous.

"*Can't?* I think you mean *won't*. You've forgotten our little agreement, haven't you, Mark?" She sounds angry; you don't know what to say to calm her down.

"Wendy, please, be reasonable."

She laughs, short and sharp. "This isn't about being reasonable, Mark. Sex isn't reasonable, and if you haven't figured that out by now, then I'm sorry for you. And I'm sorry I wasted my time with you."

"Wendy—" You can't believe that's it, that she's going to walk away.

"It's over, Mark. Good-bye." There's a dreadful finality in her voice. She hangs up the phone, leaving you to wonder, should you have done things differently? Was there some way to avoid ending up here, alone again? Or was it for the best—were you heading down a dangerous road that would have put you completely in her power, in her hands?

You'll never know now. You'll go to work tomorrow, you'll bury yourself in your books, you'll try to forget Wendy Lake. You've reached . . .

THE END

Y ou stop in at the department on the way, pick up some books from your office, send an e-mail to Wendy: *Had a terrific time at your party—looking forward to more. Much more.—Mark.* Then you walk the rest of the way home, whistling. It's good to be you.

When you get back to your apartment, you settle down to do some research—you've been slacking off a bit, and you don't want to lose this job. You quickly become immersed in the medieval world of solitary monks, isolated in their separate cells. It's a fascinating contrast with your own life; you wonder how they survived the isolation. Around three, the phone rings, yanking you reluctantly back to modern times.

"Want to come over?" Her voice is friendly, with a hint of seduction.

You hate to say it, but you have to be firm with yourself. "I need to work this afternoon, Wendy."

She chuckles softly. "Do you need to work tonight?"

You want to get your work done, but that doesn't mean you have to be a monk yourself. If you work steadily for the rest of the day, you can see Wendy tonight, come back, work all day tomorrow. You should be fine, as long as you stick to the plan. You might go short on sleep, but you're young, you can handle that.

"I could be free tonight." You smile, anticipating. "What did you have in mind?"

"A surprise. Why don't you come by after dinner? Nine would be good."

"Sounds good to me." Sounds great—that way you can work through dinner, too, grab a sandwich or something. "I'll see you then."

You hang up the phone and crack open the books. It's not long before you're buried in medieval Latin and enjoying yourself again. It's been a long time since you've had fun with this stuff—maybe all the sex will do your academic life some good, too.

You reach a stopping place with just enough time to shower and shave before catching the subway down to Wendy's neighborhood. You exchange a friendly nod with the doorman; he knows you by now. As you take the elevator up, you've got a bit of a headache from the hours at the computer, but you're also very satisfied with the amount of work you've gotten done. You body is itching for some movement. You're restless, energetic. Sitting in a chair twelve hours a day will do that to a guy.

The elevator opens to reveal Wendy, dressed in a black bra and panties. The panties have tiny bow ties on the sides. If you pull them, they'll fall right off. She's also holding something in each hand—in her right hand, black leather cuffs, fur-lined. In her left hand, a small leather whip.

"Hey, Mark. Pick one." Her face is intent, utterly serious. You don't think "neither" is likely to be an option.

- *If you choose the cuffs,* PLEASE TURN TO PAGE 224.

- *If you choose the whip,* PLEASE TURN TO PAGE 229.

Maybe you could juggle them both, but you're not willing to risk the chance of losing Sarah, or of hurting her. And maybe you take a certain satisfaction in being the man who turned down the famous Wendy Lake. Twice.

You stand up, spilling Wendy's foot out of your lap; she staggers for a second before catching her balance again.

"I'm sorry, Wendy. I could help you, but I'm not interested." You step past and open the door for her.

Wendy's pale skin turns almost white. "Don't lie to me, Mark. Your body is *quite* interested." The words are, just barely, not loud enough to be heard in the hallway. You're tired of Wendy Lake and her sexual power games.

"My body might be interested. But I'm not. Good-bye, Professor Lake."

Wendy hisses through her teeth—you've never heard a human being make a sound like that. Then she stalks out of your office and down the hall. You can't resist leaning out for one last comment: "And have a nice weekend!"

Then you gather up your books and papers and your bag. You leave your office and close the door; you walk down the hallway, whistling.

It's Friday afternoon, and Sarah is waiting.

THE END

Y ou don't say a word, you just move over Wendy's body. She spreads her legs; you slide down to your knees and dive in. This is where you want to be.

The next few weeks aren't all that different—classes during the day and occasionally seeing Wendy in the evenings. But once the semester ends, everything changes. Sometimes Wendy wants you in the morning or the afternoon—you learn to be ready whenever she calls. Oh, you could say no. Tell her you'd rather read a book instead, or take a walk in the park. But it's not like she's asking for anything onerous; she wants you to come have sex with her, which is a lot more fun than a walk in the park.

When you please her, she gives you gifts. A gold watch. Silk shirts, Prada suits. A diamond stud—she has you pierce your left nipple for that one. Sometimes she gives you money. Hundred-dollar bills pulled out of her purse, stuffed in your pants as you're dressing. You wear your fancy clothes and go out, flirting with women in hot clubs, eating in fine restaurants, shopping at Barneys. The salesclerks get to know you there. It's nice to feel rich—though when you come back to your dingy apartment at the end of the day, the illusion vanishes.

It makes you uneasy when you're paying the rent with her money, buying fresh fruit and veggies, steaks for your fridge instead of ramen for the cupboard. What will you do if she gets tired of you? She could stay interested in you for a long time, maybe forever. Or she could drop you tomorrow.

Please flip a coin.

- IF HEADS, PLEASE TURN TO PAGE 17.
- IF TAILS, PLEASE TURN TO PAGE 22.

Wendy calls you Sunday night, when you're buried deep in your work, a slice of pizza in one hand, a pen in the other. You put down the pen and pick up the phone.

"What are you doing, Mark?"

Your eyes are still on the notes, the lines of Latin you'd copied down that afternoon. You're distracted. "Reviewing some manuscript notes—did you know that our library has an amazing rare-book collection? They make you put on those silly white gloves, but it's worth it, to be able to look at, to touch the originals—"

"Mark." Wendy's voice is sharp, unamused. You realize that she wasn't really asking what you were doing. You put down the slice of pizza, push the notes aside, redirect your attention.

"Sorry. I was thinking about you."

She chuckles. "No, you weren't. But you are now, aren't you?" Her voice is soft, caressing. You wonder what she's wearing. Is she wearing anything? You're wearing an old pair of boxers yourself—September in New York is pretty warm. You imagine Wendy in an old T-shirt, faded and thin, and a pair of skimpy white cotton undies. Your cock stirs in your boxers.

"Yes. Yes, I am."

"I want you to touch yourself, Mark. Touch your cock. Will you do that for me?"

The sound of her voice saying "cock" is enough to make yours jump in your shorts. You slide a hand inside the loose waistband to touch and then stroke your cock. You must make some small sound, because the next thing Wendy says is "Good. Good boy. Stroke it for me. Stroke it until it's nice and hard." Her voice is low, intimate. You've never heard a woman say anything like this to you—it's incredibly arousing. You're already hard, so you just stroke yourself, not saying anything, until Wendy speaks again.

"Now I want you do something else for me, Mark. I want you to lick your finger, lick it all over . . . and then push it up your ass."

You could resist, say no. You resisted in her office when she wanted to do this to you. But now you're here, alone in the privacy of your apartment. Would it feel good, what she's suggesting? Everything else she's done to you has felt good—it's felt amazing.

You pull your hand out of your shorts, lick it the way she told you to. And then you reach down into your shorts again, sliding your palm over the sensitive skin of your cock, your even more sensitive balls, spreading your legs and reaching between them, underneath, until your wet finger is pressed right there, against your asshole. It feels strange—sort of tingly. Good, though. So despite a brief flutter of nervousness in your stomach, you keep going . . . you push against it, push inside. You're leaning back in your chair, tilted, with your legs braced against the tabletop, your thighs spread wide. Your finger is moving deeper and deeper into your ass, and it feels good—it feels really good. It's sending shivers through you; you can't help it. You brace the phone between your shoulder and ear, then spit on your other hand and bring it down to grab your cock. That feels even better, as you start to rub your cock with a finger deep inside your own ass.

"Good boy," Wendy says, and laughs softly. "I think you can take it from here." And she clicks off, leaving you with a dead receiver. For a brief moment, you start to get angry, but the sensations from your cock and ass are too good to sustain anger. You let the phone drop and get back to the serious business of jerking off, one hand moving quickly over the length of your cock, while the other moves a tiny bit, in and out of your ass. It doesn't take long at all before you're coming all over your shorts.

You don't hear from Wendy for the rest of the week; you don't see her in the department, either. You can't call her—her number is unlisted. You're lying in your narrow bed the following Friday night, the next time she calls. You had been considering the cracks on your ceiling and realizing that with the last phone call, Wendy started taking control again. If you're not careful, she'll begin ordering you around all the time—and even if the things she tells you to do feel good, really good, you can't let her call all the shots.

What kind of a man are you if you're letting a woman lead you around by the dick? It's time for you to be more aggressive; it's time to tell her what to do for a change. She might like it. She might like it a lot. Of course, she might drop you at the suggestion. She's unpredictable that way.

The phone rings once, twice, while you consider this. You pick it up on the third ring. You know it's her.

"Hello, Wendy."

"Do you want to come over and lick my pussy, Mark?" Her voice is light, teasing, seductive. She sounds like she's in a good mood. Why shouldn't she be in a good mood? She always gets what she wants from you.

You're irritated, but you try to keep your tone light. Teasing, to match hers. You don't want to let her know this matters to you. "Actually, Wendy, I'm more in the mood to fuck you tonight. When I come over tonight, why don't I just sink my cock into your sweet cunt?"

"You're joking." All traces of good humor, of emotion, have been wiped away from her voice. You can't read her—she sounds entirely flat. Is she annoyed? Upset? Simply incredulous?

You clear your throat. "Not at all." You load your voice with promise, with every ounce of seduction you can manage. Seductiveness isn't something you've had much practice at. "I had gotten the impression you rather liked it when I fucked you. You certainly sounded like you did. Isn't that right? Have I been under a misapprehension?"

"Are you sure you want to do this, Mark?" There's almost a threat in those words, and then Wendy's voice regains its teasing, inviting flavor. "If you come over and lick me, then I might suck you off. Afterward." She wants you, but she wants you on her terms. If you keep pushing, you might lose her entirely. Your head has started to ache with the frustration of this conversation. If it goes on much longer, you might not want to have any kind of sex at all.

- *If you want to make a point,* PLEASE TURN TO PAGE 204.

- *If you give up on the idea and go over to her place as usual,* PLEASE TURN TO PAGE 169.

"You've got to be joking." You might lose her, but you can't simply do what she wants. "Be reasonable, Wendy. I could get arrested. Ask me for something else." This has been fascinating, fun, and you want to keep pleasing her, but there are limits. There have to be limits.

Wendy is silent for a moment, and then she starts to laugh. It's an odd sound—high-pitched, brittle. But she doesn't sound angry. "You're tired of our little game, then? Well, perhaps it was losing its charm." She's quiet again, thinking, perhaps. And then she says, "Just come over, Mark. Come over and fuck me."

You swallow a sigh of relief. You don't want her to know that you were worried. "I'll be there in twenty minutes."

You strip, shower, and dress again in less than ten. You grab your wallet, then stop long enough to count the cash in it. You have enough for a cab, but only if you skip lunch for the next two days. It'll be worth it; you don't have the patience to deal with the subway. You take a cab over to her apartment. She meets you at the door, takes your hand, leads you to the bedroom, and takes off your clothes. You fuck her there for hours. In the bed, on the floor, up against the wall. In the shower, the Jacuzzi tub. Back in the bed. She's demanding, inexhaustible, and somehow you manage to keep up. It's almost sunrise when you finally start to fall asleep. She shakes you, wakes you up.

"Go home, Mark."

She's going to send you home now? But you're so tired. "I thought I could just crash here."

"I don't let anyone sleep with me. It's a cardinal rule. You're a nice boy, Mark, but I'm not about to make an exception for you. Go home."

You stagger out of bed and manage to get dressed. She's asleep before you finish, sprawled across the entire bed. You take the subway home in the early Saturday morning—the cab took all your cash, and you're lucky to find a token in your pants pocket. You're a little dazed, more than a little exhausted. But you're exhilarated, too; it's intoxicating, fucking Wendy Lake.

• PLEASE TURN TO PAGE 198.

I'm sure, Wendy. Fucking or nothing tonight. Do you want it?" You aren't sure, but you can fake it.

"Okay, okay—we'll fuck. Fine." Wendy sounds exasperated, but not actually angry. You take a risk and push for a little bit more.

"And Wendy, why don't you come over here tonight? For a change?" You hold your breath, waiting for her answer.

There's a startled silence on the other end of the line, and then Wendy starts laughing. You relax, but only fractionally, until she stops laughing and says, "I'll be there in twenty minutes." Wendy Lake hangs up the phone, and you feel a mix of triumph and apprehension. You've got her, but do you know what to do with her?

You spend the next twenty minutes frantically getting ready— showering and shaving and straightening up, throwing clothes into the closet, moving books from the bed to the floor. You can't do anything about the cockroaches. The sheets are clean, at least. That's something. You don't bother to dress.

When Wendy arrives, you give her only a minute to glance around before you reach out and pull her into a kiss. Keep her on the defensive—that's the trick. As long as she keeps reacting to what you're doing, then she won't have time to get critical, to take back control. You kiss her hard, your hands pressing against the small of her back, pulling her against you. She freezes for a moment, then gives in, kissing you with equal intensity, her tongue darting out to meet yours, tangling with it. It feels more like a battle than a kiss. You push her back onto the narrow bed, kissing her mouth, her throat. You unbutton her dress, pale blue, sprigged with tiny white flowers, incongruously innocent. You kiss the valley between her breasts. You pull down the cups of her black lace bra, freeing her breasts, licking and then suckling on the nipples—first the right, then the left. She arches underneath you, her fingers loosely tangled in your hair, apparently content to let you run this show.

You're trying to be careful, to be skilled, as you move farther down her body. But your dick is hard, and you can't seem to think straight. She smells incredible, like spring rain. You're having trouble with the buttons of her dress; she reaches down and undoes them for you. You bite her stomach, her thighs. Your mouth closes briefly over her naked cunt, and she whimpers, but you can't linger there, you need more. You need to bury your cock inside her. You surge up over her body. You push apart her legs with yours and find her cunt with your cock. You thrust hard, pushing deep inside her. Her hands come up; her nails dig into your back as you fuck her, fuck her against the battered mattress, the creaking springs. Has Wendy Lake ever fucked in a place as ugly, as pathetic, as this? She seems to like it here; she's whimpering, begging you to fuck her more, harder, longer. And you do—you feel full of energy, strength, you feel like you could fuck her for months, or years. And she's biting your neck, she's moaning, screaming, collapsing against the bed. But you're not done, and you fuck her more and more, fuck her through orgasm after orgasm until you come, too, with a feeling of triumph that makes the pleasure even better, better than it's ever been before.

Afterward, Wendy tries to pretend nothing's changed. She gets up from the bed, buttons her dress over the bruised, bitten flesh, walks out without even a word. But everything's different now. Wendy wants you, wants you badly enough to come here, to this disgusting hole that you're forced to live in. And, fine, you want her, too. Want her desperately. No argument there. But at least it goes both ways.

In the next few weeks, you both go to your classes, do your work.

She's publishing another popular book; she's doing a lot of publicity, TV and radio interviews. Wendy's face is all over the press; when you walk by the newsstand, she jumps out at you from magazine covers. It's exciting, being involved with a celebrity.

Your own research is picking up speed. What you had thought was going to be only an article on a particularly obscure medieval monk is turning more interesting; you're making connections with some broader patterns in the Church. You think you may be able to get a book out of it. If you can, that'll probably guarantee you the tenure-track job. When you see Benjamin in the hallways, he smiles encouragingly at you. The department is a happy place to be.

You're both working well, working hard. And at night . . . at night you're playing hard. You're pushing each other, trying new things. You're alternating between your place and hers, and if the contrast in environment is great, the contrast in Wendy is greater.

When you're at her place, she takes charge. She tells you what to do, when and where to do it. She tells you exactly how she wants you to fuck her—slow and tender, or fast and hard and unrelenting. She tells you to lick her pussy, to stick your fingers up her cunt, to spank her ass until it's red and your hand is aching. And you don't mind following her orders, because you know that the next night, at your place, you're going to be the one in charge.

If you tell her to suck your cock for hours, you know she will. She'll let you come all over her face, or in her ass. She tells you how much she wants you, how much she needs you. How she's getting addicted to you. And maybe you're getting addicted to her. You can tell it bothers her, wanting you like this. She's used to being in control with her lovers. But there must be something about you that she really likes, because she keeps coming back for more.

In the middle of October, the heart of the semester, Wendy calls you late at night, asks you to come over. There's something strange in her voice.

You take the subway to her apartment, wave at the doorman, and take the elevator upstairs. You walk through the apartment to the bedroom only to find another man there, in her bed, fucking her. He's a skinny guy with a hairy chest; the room is filled with his sweaty odor. They've been fucking for a while. Wendy lifts her head off the pillow, turns it, smiles at you. For a brief moment, you want to strangle her, strangle them both. It's like a knife in the guts, and you can't help flashing back to that scene last May, Sarah's legs wrapped around some strange man's ass.

You could break this guy in half. But there's a strange clarity within you. You know there's no way that Wendy really wanted a loser like this. This is all for your benefit, it's all a show, meant to make you mad, make you crazy, make you react, so she can be the one in charge again. Realizing that gives you the strength *not* to react. To freeze for a second, expressionless, and then to deliberately shrug, to turn, to walk out and walk away. You don't call her for weeks. You avoid her at the office and ignore her messages.

It isn't easy—in fact, it's torture. You've gotten used to regular sex, and you have to bury yourself in work to do it at all. But you do it, and when you finally call her, when you tell her to come over to your apartment, she comes obediently, apologetically. She sucks you on her knees, over and over again.

→

Late on that following Saturday, you're sprawled out on Wendy's massive bed, with her resting against your chest in a rare moment of peace. You're still catching your breath—you've exhausted yourself tonight. That always seems to be the way with her; you push each other, further and further. It's exhilarating but also tiring. Sometimes you wish you could relax instead of always needing to impress her, compete with her.

Wendy says, "What do you think about other women?"

"In what context?" You're cautious—you think you know what she's asking, but better to be sure.

"Do you want to *have sex* with other women?" She says the words slowly, enunciating clearly.

You don't let her get to you. "I repeat, in what context?"

Wendy says, "There's a friend of mine. I think you'd like her. I've told her all about you, and she wants to meet you."

You're immediately curious—what has Wendy has been telling her friends about you? But that isn't the important question. "You wouldn't mind?" You certainly minded walking in on her and that guy, although that was partly because you knew she was doing it to make you mad.

Wendy shrugs. "Why would I mind?"

It's every guy's dream, isn't it? A girlfriend who'll let you sleep with other women. Part of you isn't inclined to question, but after her little power play before, you don't want to accept it blindly, either.

"Does that mean you'll get to have sex with other men?"

"And women. Wouldn't that be fair?" Wendy smiles.

Your brain got stuck on that "and women" part. You're imagining Wendy and another woman, women, all naked and tangled up on this lovely big bed. You try to drag your mind back to the idea of her with a man. How much would that bother you, really? You're not in love with her—you don't think. Wendy would be a dangerous woman to be in love with. Does it matter if she sleeps with other men? "And I'd have to watch this?"

She raises an eyebrow at you. "If you want to. You don't have to. It's entirely up to you whether you come to the party."

"What party?" Now you're confused—you'd thought you were talking about inviting somebody over here to join you in bed. Where did a party come into it?

"I always have a sex party on Halloween. It's a tradition. That's where you'd hook up with Rhonda, if you want to."

Rhonda. You try to imagine a Rhonda and fail. You can't imagine a sex party, either, but you know one thing: you don't want Wendy having one without you there. It sounds like Wendy's planning on having the party whether or not you attend, so you might as well go and see what happens.

"I can't promise anything until I see her. But I'll come to the party, and we can see what happens then."

Wendy smiles again and rolls over. "Sounds good," she says sleepily. You can tell by the sound of her voice that she'll be fast asleep soon, which means it's your cue to get up, get dressed, and go. That much hasn't changed, at any rate—she still never lets you spend the night.

• PLEASE TURN TO PAGE 23.

"Wendy, I can't do it." You swing out of the bed and start getting dressed. You're waiting for her to call you back, to persuade you to stay—but she just lies there, watching you. Maybe she doesn't care whether you stay or go. That makes the decision easier: you have to go. And go now, before you're utterly at her mercy. You're not sure Wendy Lake has any mercy to spare.

You finish getting dressed and leave the apartment. You walk home, a thickness filling up your throat. You've lost everything for a woman who couldn't care less about you. What are you going to do now?

The next few months are painful. No one seems to be hiring in the city, or at least not for anything you're qualified for. You're not sure what you're qualified for, honestly. Something to do with books, with words. But the bookstores don't want you, and neither do the magazines or newspapers. You have to call your mother for rent money. She wants you to come home to Chicago, but you don't ever want to be in that city again. If you go back there, you know you'll end up calling Sarah and starting that whole mess over.

Wendy Lake seems to have lost interest in you entirely. Once you turned down her offer, she stopped calling you and stopped picking up your calls. You leave a series of increasingly unhappy messages on her machine, but you finally stop before you lose your last shreds of self-respect. Maybe she was interested only in playing games with you, interested only in fucking people whose lives she could truly fuck with. Whatever. You can manage fine without her.

You do eventually get a bottom-level job at a publishing house, as a production editor. You get paid a measly $27,500 and have to move out to New Jersey in order to afford an apartment. You have a painful commute, but you're working, and working with books. Maybe someday you'll have a real job, something you can be proud of. In the meantime, at least you're paying your own way. That's something.

And it's not all hopeless. There's a cute intern from NYU at the publishing house, a friendly redhead. Suzanne is open, vivacious, cheerful, the total opposite of Wendy Lake. And she seems to actually like you. You're going to ask her out one of these days. Soon. And then you'll be able to have a normal boyfriend-girlfriend relationship again. You're sure she'll appreciate all the sexual tricks you learned from Wendy Lake. When you look at it right, Wendy did you a favor. It wasn't easy leaving academia, but it seems you weren't suited to it anyway. Your involvement with Wendy helped make that clear.

Really, it all worked out fine in . . .

THE END

It's late November when it happens, a few weeks before final exams. A young girl, Ruth Epstein, lingers after office hours on a Friday afternoon. She's barely seventeen—a bright young prodigy who came to college a year early. Ruth is clearly fascinated by you, in the way that young women so often are by slightly older men. She's been acing your class all semester, but she comes to your office hours every time you hold them. Ruth stands too close to you; she leans in, so you can't help catching the scent of her hair, her skin. And while she would never have the nerve to ask out her professor, you know in your gut, your groin, that if you approached her, she wouldn't say no. She wouldn't know how.

You know it's wrong. She's your student. You're her teacher. But it's hard to think about ethics when she's sitting across from you in your tiny office, her bare knees almost touching yours. Ruth has taken off her coat; she's wearing a white button-down cardigan, a short blue skirt, thick knee-high socks—the picture of an innocent schoolgirl. You're sure she is innocent, that she's never had a man touch her, not really. Oh, maybe a few fumbled kisses in high school, but now she's in college. And if she's not careful, she'll soon be seduced by some clumsy jock who doesn't know what the hell he's doing and doesn't much care, as long as he gets to stick his dick into some hot young pussy. You could do so much better for her; you could teach her how glorious sex can be. She'd enjoy herself, you'd make sure of that.

It'd mean cheating on Wendy, but it's not as if Wendy is being faithful to you. You're having fun with Wendy, but you can't stop thinking about how satisfying it would be to be the one in control again, the one running the show. Ruth knows nothing, you could teach her everything. Teach her to enjoy a man's touch. Teach her to touch a man in the ways he most enjoys. Teach her to kiss you, to lick and suck you, exactly the way you like it. You're her teacher, after all.

Ruth leans forward, and her small pink tongue darts out to lick her lips. Your balls tighten and your cock pulses.

• *If you try to seduce Ruth,* PLEASE TURN TO THE NEXT PAGE.

• *If you decide not to,* PLEASE TURN TO PAGE 172.

It's better not to try to talk. Talking would only confuse things. Instead, you get up, walk over to the door, close it firmly, turn the key in the lock.

"Professor?" Ruth is standing up, confused. But not suspicious—she's so sweet that she still trusts you. Trusts you with her fair young body.

You take a single step, put your arms around her, and pull her into a kiss. Your mouth is urgent on hers, but gentle. One of your hands is on her back, pulling her close; the other is on the nape of her neck, applying soft pressure to keep her there, trapped in your arms. She freezes at first, but you continue kissing her, your mouth moving on her skin, her lips. You're very gentle—you don't want to scare the girl. You want her willing and eager in your arms. It isn't long before Ruth starts kissing you back, a whimper in the back of her throat, her hands pressed helplessly against your chest, between your bodies. Her small, pointed breasts are crushed against you, and when your mouth leaves her, sliding down to her bare neck, she only shivers and tilts her head back, surrendering to you.

You unbutton each tiny button of her blouse to reveal a thin white cotton bra. You kiss her breasts through the fabric, lingering on each small nipple until it's hard against your wet, moving mouth. Ruth's hands are moving lightly in your hair, tiny, frantic movements, like fluttering moths. She's arching under your touch, her slender body curving up to meet you. You keep moving down, kissing her bare stomach, her navel. You reach down and gather her blue skirt in your hands, pulling the fabric up, baring—of course—white cotton panties, devoid of lace or ribbons. Simple and plain and beautiful.

You slide a hand inside her panties. Ruth is wet, and her pussy clenches around your probing fingers. She's shivering, biting her lip to keep quiet, but you can feel how aroused she is, how ready. She's been fantasizing about her handsome professor for weeks, never imagining that he would ever want her. But he does. He very much does. You give her one last kiss, then turn her around, bending her over your desk. You pull her panties down; they fall to her ankles. Then you undo your pants, free your cock. You apply gentle pressure to her thighs, and she moves them apart for you. You press the head of your cock against her wet opening, then push in. She's tighter than Wendy, tighter than anywhere you've ever been.

You push in, slowly, gently. You don't want to hurt the girl, not more than is needful. You kiss the soft nape of her neck; you rub your hands across her breasts, squeezing the nipples. Ruth is making little noises, and you can't tell if they're pain or pleasure, but she's also pushing back against you, urging you on. So you keep pushing in until you hit a barrier, and then you push farther, tearing through, and she's gasping, but you keep kissing her, keep your hands moving across her skin. As you start to pump slowly in and out, she begins to respond again, to arch back against you, to whimper softly in pleasure. And Ruth feels incredible—slick and hot and almost painfully tight.

It comes close to being too much; you almost squirt right then and there, but that wouldn't be fair to the girl. You could do that to Wendy, but a sweet innocent like this deserves more than that. So you hold back, you don't let yourself pound her the way you'd like to. You lick your fingers and bring them down to rub her clit, you whisper in her ear as you slowly fuck her. You tell her that she's beautiful, that you couldn't resist her, that you've been thinking about her all semester, all year, ever since she walked into your classroom. It's all true, or true enough, and it turns her on; she's humping your hand, moving faster, sliding up and down on your cock, and you hardly have to do anything. She's learning what feels good, what feels amazingly good, and she's getting closer and closer until she comes, comes hard in spasms around your cock, and that does it—that's all you can take, and you come, too, squirting deep inside her no-longer-virginal young pussy, coming with deep shudders of pleasure that rack your entire body.

Afterward, she asks if she can see you again, do this again. You tell her yes. How can you say no? It would be cruel.

Your life becomes incredibly satisfying. You're still having a terrific time with Wendy, and on the nights when Wendy doesn't call you, you call Ruth. She comes over to your apartment, and you screw on your dingy bed. Her body is so beautifully young, so taut and slender. You sink your cock into her pussy again and again—though after that first time, you make sure you're both using protection. You're lucky you didn't get her pregnant that first time; you really would have been screwed then. You love fucking her. You revel in the sheer sensations of touching Ruth's delicate, perfect skin, her firm breasts.

Even more satisfying is the way she treats you. She thinks you're glorious, brilliant, a sex god. It doesn't matter how lazy you are, how carelessly you touch her—she's in a constant fever of arousal, and your slightest caress can make her whimper. Ruth loves sucking your cock, licking your balls, even your ass, once you convince her that you'll enjoy it. She's desperately eager to please you. She's sweet, she's submissive, she can't get enough of you. It's perfection—until it all falls apart.

You're lying back on the bed, with Ruth still dressed, kneeling between your legs, about to take your dick in her small mouth, when Wendy walks in.

"Wendy! I thought you had other plans tonight." You're pulling a sheet up to cover yourself. Ruth's jumping off the bed, one hand coming up to cover her mouth.

Wendy stands in the doorway, still in her coat. "I wanted to surprise you." She smiles kindly at Ruth. "Who are you, sweetheart?"

"Professor Lake!" Ruth blurts out.

Wendy shakes her head gently. "No, I'm Professor Lake. And you must be one of Mark's students."

Ruth reaches out to touch your shoulder, and you reach up to touch her hand with yours. "Mark isn't doing anything wrong! We're in love!" You feel a brief pang of contrition; you'd never told the silly girl that you loved her, but perhaps you should have known what she would think. You squeeze her hand once, then let go. You know Wendy isn't going to let that little statement pass.

Wendy doesn't disappoint you. "Oh, sweetheart. I'm Mark's girlfriend, not you, honey. I've been having sex with Mark for months. Every other night or so. He only had sex with you when I wasn't available. Isn't that right, Mark?"

You don't know what to say. You can't tell if Wendy is angry or amused. And since when is she your *girlfriend*? It doesn't matter what you say or don't say; Ruth turns to you and sees the truth on your face. Tears well up in her eyes and start running down her cheeks.

"Oh, don't cry over him, dear. He's not worth it. We'll go talk to the dean tomorrow. Wouldn't you like to see Mark punished for lying to you, for taking advantage of his position of power?" Wendy's eyes glitter in the dim light. You can't believe she would take this to the dean. Why would she do this to you?

"But Wendy—Ruth!"

Ruth wipes the tears from her eyes and crosses the room to stand next to Wendy. "I would love to."

Wendy pats her shoulder. "That's good, dear. Now, would you do me a favor? Go wait downstairs in the lobby. I'll come down in a minute and give you a ride home."

Ruth nods and picks up her coat. She walks out the door without looking back at you, leaving you alone with Wendy Lake.

You swing your legs off the bed and stand up, still clutching the sheet around you. You feel ridiculous, but it would be worse to be naked with Wendy Lake there, fully dressed, still in her overcoat.

"Wendy, you aren't really going to do this to me, are you? This is just one of your little games . . . what do you want me to do now? Whatever it is, I'll do it—just don't get me fired!" You take a step forward, pleading. Now isn't the time to stand on pride.

"I'm not going to do anything to you, Mark. I'm not going to get you fired." You start to sigh in relief, but before you can, Wendy continues, stepping forward into the room, reaching out and taking your chin in her hand. "You did this to yourself. You're getting yourself fired." She turns your chin to the side, and you yank it away when you realize that she's *inspecting* it. Looking for character flaws?

She continues, looking you up and down. "I'm surprised that I misjudged you so badly. I knew you were somewhat lacking in spine, Mark, but I didn't realize what a weak, pathetic person you are. Taking advantage of one of your students, a *child*—is that girl even eighteen?" The guilt must be written plainly on your face. "I didn't think so." She looks utterly disgusted.

What right does she have to be disgusted? After everything you know she's done. "But Wendy, I thought you'd understand. You and I, everything we've done together." All the men and women she's fucked, she should understand why you couldn't resist sweet, willing Ruth. "She wanted to fuck me, Wendy. She wanted it badly!"

Wendy shakes her head. "You still don't get it. We're adults, Mark. Consenting adults, and whatever we choose to do is our business and nobody else's. Except those other consenting adults whom we might choose to invite to join us."

Now you're getting angry. She's up on some high horse; that can't be what this is about. "This is mere jealousy. You're upset that I was fucking another woman—a younger woman, too. That's what this is about." You intend to go on, to tell her that you never loved Ruth, that all you ever wanted was more time with Wendy, on equal terms. But she cuts you off before you can continue.

"Mark, I couldn't care less who you fuck. You could've fucked half the female professors on campus, and I wouldn't have blinked an eye, even if they were ten years younger than me. But an underage girl, and to make it worse, a student of yours—I'm going to take pleasure in seeing you fired so that you can never abuse your position again. And I plan on that being the last I ever see of you." She turns then and walks out the door, pulling it closed behind her.

You want to go after her, to pull her back, to explain. But no explanations will help you now—you're finished with Ruth, with Wendy Lake, with your career. You stand there in your dirty bedsheet, knowing in your gut that you've finally reached a miserable, pathetic . . .

THE END

"Is your car here?" Everyone in the department knows about her red BMW. Wendy nods, her long black hair falling forward across her face, shadowing those ice-blue eyes. You feel a sudden pulse of desire shoot through you. You don't know what it is about this woman, but she makes it hard to think.

"Go wait for me in the faculty lot. Take off your panties when you get in the car. I'll meet you in a few minutes." You expect her to argue, but she strokes your cock one last time with her foot, then slides her shoe back on and walks out the door. You take a deep breath, reach over to your phone. You call Sarah.

"Sweetheart, I'm sorry—I forgot all about a fellowship deadline. I'm going to have to go to the library and get some materials, then work like crazy for the next few hours if I'm going to file it on time. Can I get a rain check just this once? I'll be home by seven, and I promise to make it up to you tonight."

And then you're free to go find Wendy Lake, waiting with a bare pussy in her cherry-red BMW.

When you get out to the car, Wendy is waiting for you in the tiny backseat.

"Not here," you say. It's way too dangerous to screw in the parking lot. Much too easy to get caught—and getting caught is definitely not part of your plans. Wendy looks surprised but tosses you her keys. You slide into the driver's seat. Wendy climbs up into the front passenger's side, her long legs slipping through the narrow well between the seats. You reach over and slide the fabric of her skirt up, enough to check her cunt. It's bare, available to you, as instructed. You slide your fingers in and out a few times, getting her wet. She starts to press against your fingers, to whimper. You take your hand away. "Buckle up," you say, and she does. You buckle your own seat belt and start the car.

You drive for twenty minutes or so, until you're in an area you don't recognize, a part of the city Sarah's never been to, either. You park in a Holiday Inn parking lot, get out of the car, and lead Wendy to the front desk. She pays for the room under her own name. The attendant doesn't blink an eye—why should he? On the surface, there's nothing suspicious. You're entirely discreet.

You wait until you're safely in the bedroom before you strip off your clothes, strip Wendy of hers. You're kissing her, your hands buried in that long fall of silken hair. Your naked bodies are pressed together, and you want her, want her badly enough that you don't even make it over to the bed. You're falling to the floor, spreading her legs apart with yours, your hard cock poised over her pussy.

Wendy says, "But what about poor Sarah?" Her voice is wicked, taunting.

You drive your cock deep into Wendy, eliciting a startled moan. As you start to fuck her, slowly, you say, "What Sarah doesn't know won't hurt her. And she's never going to know, is she, Wendy? Because if she ever does find out, if you ever tell her, you won't get to fuck me anymore, and I know you want it. You want it bad." Wendy doesn't deny it. She just wraps her legs around you and shoves her pussy up to meet you until you're slamming your hips together in ecstatic rhythm.

You fuck her on the floor, her head thumping back against it. When Wendy starts to scratch your back, you reach behind you and grab her hands. No inexplicable marks on your body. But in the hours of fucking that follow, you mark her—you suck hickeys on her neck, her pale breasts. You scratch her back. You leave bite marks on the soft flesh of her inner thighs. You fuck her until she's wincing at the soreness of her cunt, and then you roll her over and fuck her ass.

At six-thirty, you get up and shower. At six-forty, Wendy puts you in a cab and pays the fare. She kisses you hard before you close the taxi door.

Coming home is tricky. You hesitate with your key in the door, not quite ready to turn it. How good an actor are you? Can you fool her?

You won't know until you try. You turn the key and step into the apartment.

Sarah's in the kitchen, cooking dinner. You can smell grilled pepper steak, roast potatoes. It's your traditional Friday dinner; she says it keeps your strength up. Now you have to fake it—you've exhausted yourself fucking all afternoon, but Sarah thinks you've been working. If you want to keep her from getting suspicious, you'll have to make love to her the way she expects you to, with passion and energy and intensity. Luckily, you're fully capable of doing that all night long.

"Hey, sweetheart." She's running down the short hallway, throwing her arms around you; you pull her up into a hug. "Did you miss me?"

"Always," you answer as you bend down for a passionate kiss. She tastes like honey and sunshine. You feel a quick surge of affection for her. You bury your face in her blond hair for a moment. A kitchen timer rings, and she squirms out of your arms, heading back down the hall. "Sorry, gotta get that," she calls over her shoulder. "More of the fun stuff after dinner, okay?"

You follow her into the kitchen, start helping with the salad, rinsing lettuce. She glances over at you and smiles; her smile lights up her whole face.

Between Sarah's sweet loving and Wendy's crazy fucking, you've somehow lucked in to every man's dream—two gorgeous women, both of whom love having sex with you. Your grad school buddies would never believe it—it's too bad you'll never be able to tell them. Only in New York could you pull this off. Somehow you've found the perfect happy ending.

THE END

You reach out and touch her right hand. You're not certain what you're letting yourself in for, but it should be interesting. And you wouldn't mind having her direct things for a while; you can lie back and see where she takes you.

She nods, then leads you through her large apartment to her bedroom. It's a very sleek room—all silvery grays, quite dramatic. Cold, too. But that's okay with you.

"Strip," she says quietly. You take off your clothes, and soon you're standing naked before her. She steps forward, places her long hands on your chest, and pushes gently so that you fall back onto the bed. You have to fight down a giggle; it's hard to take this as seriously as the role demands.

"Roll over and put your hands above your head." You roll over onto your stomach and obey, and she climbs over your prone body, reaching to fasten the cuffs to the bed and then to your crossed wrists. It's oddly unsettling, being restrained like this; you tug at the cuffs and realize that you can't get yourself loose. She could do anything to you: could leave you here for days, could videotape you, could even cut you. You've never been so helpless as an adult, and you feel a brief moment of panic. Wendy must see it in your eyes—she smiles wickedly as she picks up a black silk scarf from the nightstand and ties it around your head, tightly enough that you can't see anything. The panic surges, but then she gently caresses the side of your face, reassuringly, until your pulse calms. You're pretty sure she isn't going to do anything that'll hurt you. You take a deep breath and force yourself to relax. Wendy puts her fingers in your mouth, urges it open. More fabric is stuffed inside your mouth; it tastes dry and makes your mouth dry, too. You try to make a small noise, experimentally. It's muffled. If you yelled, no one would hear you.

Then she slides back down, and the simple movement of her skin against yours is enough to harden your cock, trapped against the bed. Wendy comes to rest, kneeling between your thighs, and reaches down to caress your balls. It's almost ticklish, but not quite. Your cock gets even harder. Her hand slides up, checks its hardness. She must approve, because she then bends down and starts licking your ass. You're a little shocked, and more than a little embarrassed. You hadn't expected anything like this, and you wish you'd taken a longer, more careful shower; you bury your face against the sheets. But Wendy is eagerly spreading the cheeks apart to slide her tongue around your asshole, while her hand squeezes your cock firmly. She seems to be enjoying this. The sensation of her wet tongue probing your ass sends shivers through your entire body, and it isn't long before you're bucking against the bed, arching your ass up, against her mouth, wanting more.

She stops. She pulls away. She says, "Little boys who can't keep still must be punished." There's a funny note in her voice—almost as if she's stifling a giggle. You're tempted to laugh, too, but then she starts to whip you.

At first, it seems funny. It's not a very big whip, and she's not hitting you very hard. Just light, whippy blows across your ass. Your ass can take it, no problem.

Then she starts to hit harder. And parts of your ass are starting to get kind of sore; when she comes back to those bits, you can't help wincing slightly. You don't make any sound, though. Your ass is a bit warm, a bit sore, but that's all. The gag is sort of an insult, if you think about it. It's not as if she's going to hurt you.

Then she pauses—and when she starts to hit you again, everything's changed. She's switched to something heavier, harder. It doesn't feel like a whip, more like a crop or a cane. You're not sure; no one has ever hit you before. Not unless you count your mother putting you over her knee and spanking you, but that was twenty years ago, and she stopped when you started to yell. Wendy Lake doesn't show any signs of stopping. She hits you again and again, and now your ass is more than sore, it actually hurts. You shift around with each blow, trying to find some untouched area for her next blow to land on, but you're quickly running out of those. You can't see your ass—you can't see anything—but it must be bright red. Occasionally, she'll lay down a cut across your thighs, and that truly stings, makes you yelp, and you're thankful for the gag that keeps the sound from reaching Wendy's ears. Though somehow you think she probably knows.

She plays with the timing, sometimes pausing long enough that you think it's over, before laying down a sudden flurry of blows that make you whimper and arch away. You can't move very far, and somehow you don't want to try. There's a part of you that wants to lie there and take it, take as much as Wendy wants to give, make a present to her of your bound and suffering self. If this pleases her, if she enjoys your pain, then you can make it a point of pride to take as much as she can dish out, to take it and like it. Because you do like it; you can't deny that your cock is still hard, hard and aching, your balls are sore, and your whole body is wanting to fuck. This beating is turning you on, and when you're not trying to avoid the next blow, you're sinking into the sensations in your ass, your thighs. The burning, the caresses.

Sometimes she stops and runs a slender hand along your ass, pauses, and digs her nails in, and that feels good, too—or, if not good, then at least intense. Everything feels so damn intense. She reaches under and caresses your cock, too, making sure you're still turned on, still into it. You are. She's hitting harder and harder, a frenzy of blows building up to a climax, until she lays one down, hard, right along your ass crack, sending pain shooting through you so that you can't help but yell against the gag. And that's when she rolls you over, pulls her panties off, and climbs on top, her dripping cunt sliding down to engulf your insanely hard cock, climbs up and fucks you, one, two, three strokes, and that's it. You come, you come so hard that you arch up and nearly throw her off you, coming and coming until your balls are emptied and you see stars against the black of the blindfold.

Wendy sinks down, dropping a single kiss on your cheek. She wraps her arms around you and rests her body against your chest.

• PLEASE TURN TO PAGE 233.

The last thing you need is to get involved with Sarah again. All she ever brought you was grief. She was just too emotional.

Women are too much trouble; all you want to do is concentrate on your career. Get some decent work done, publish some papers, maybe a book. Get a tenure-track job with a respectable salary. If you work hard for the rest of this year, you know you can do that. Maybe later you'll have time to pursue women. For now, you're not all that interested.

THE END

You reach out and take the whip from her left hand. She smiles and hands you the cuffs as well. It's all in your hands. It's a nice feeling—so far, she's been the one in control, calling the shots. It's your turn.

"Bedroom." You're not sure yet what you want to do with your new-found power, but you know where you want to do it. Wendy obediently turns and leads you through the large apartment to her bedroom. Once inside, she turns again to face you and waits for your next move.

You like being dressed and having her wear only lingerie, but this could be even better. You reach out and unclasp her bra, pull it off, baring her small breasts. Her nipples are soft; you can fix that. But first, you reach out and pull those tiny bow ties, and the panties flutter to the floor, leaving her deliciously naked. You could tell her to give you a blow job—your cock is nice and hard—but you could also make it more interesting. This kind of game is all about power, right? And there's a particular game that could be a lot of fun to play.

"So, Miss Lake. You wanted to speak to me?"

A tiny upward twitch of Wendy Lake's mouth tells you that she's caught on. She quickly puts on a very young, very demure expression before stepping forward and saying, "Oh, Professor Matthews, I can't go home to my father and tell him I only got a B plus in your course. He'd be so angry. Please, isn't there any way I can convince you to change my grade to an A? Isn't there anything I can do for you?" She looks at you pleadingly—you can almost imagine tears welling in her eyes.

"Why, Miss Lake! I'm shocked. What exactly are you offering?" You cross your arms in front of your chest and endeavor to look stern and forbidding.

Wendy puts a hand on your crossed arms, stepping closer.

"Whatever you want, Professor Matthews. I need that A so very, very badly."

You reach out to a naked breast and tweak one of her nipples, squeezing it hard until it's firm and erect. "Miss Lake, do you think I'm the kind of man who would trade a high grade for some naughty, tawdry sex with one of his students?"

"Only if the student is very good at sucking cock, Professor. Then your student could *earn* her A." Wendy licks her lips slowly.

"Very well, Miss Lake. You may try sucking my cock. If you do a good job, then I might be able to adjust your grade slightly. It all depends on how well you perform." You sit down on the bed, facing her, the whip still casually held in one hand. "Of course, if you don't do well . . . there might be some unfortunate consequences."

"Oh, thank you, Professor! I'll do a good job, you'll see!" Wendy slides to kneel on the floor and quickly unbuttons your pants, unzipping them and pushing the fabric aside to free your cock. She bends down and takes you in her wet mouth, her long hair falling to hide her face. That's no good, so you reach out and gather it in your hand, pulling it to the nape of her neck. Oh, yeah, that's much better.

As she sucks and licks, you can adjust the movement, pulling her hair slightly or pushing at the back of her head, urging her on. She seems to like it—when you tug, her tongue moves faster, and she lets out a small sexy whimper. An aroused whimper. She really seems to be getting off on sucking your cock.

It's hard to believe she's enjoying it that much—so you pull back on her hair, pulling her off your cock and back far enough that you can see her breasts . . . and yes, her nipples are hard, sticking straight out. You want to touch them, but you also want her mouth back on your cock. You can touch them later. You let her bend forward again, and her mouth is moving faster, one hand is coming up to grasp the base of your cock, wet with saliva. Her hand is sliding up and down the base, in rhythm with her moving mouth, and her other hand is cupping your balls; her whimpers are getting louder, and all of the sensations combine to send the come spurting up, out of you, into her eager mouth. She pulls away at the very last spurt, enough so that some of it spurts across her mouth, and then she sits back on her heels, naked, with your come on her face, waiting to see what you thought.

"Well. That wasn't bad, Miss Lake. Not bad at all. I think that earns you an A minus, right there." You smile benignly down at her. You're fighting to stifle a laugh—it's surprisingly hard to keep up the act. But if she won't break character, you're determined not to, either.

Wendy pouts. It's silly, but kind of cute, too. The expression makes her look ten years younger—she really could be an undergrad. "But professor, I really need an A. Are you *sure* that wasn't an A-level blow job? Maybe even an A plus?"

You chuckle. "I'm sorry, Miss. You're going to have to be satisfied with an A minus. I'm not one of those easy graders you hear about; you have to earn an A in my class."

Wendy suddenly grins, then stands up, plucking the whip from your hand and dropping it to the floor. "Then I'd better try harder, don't you think?" And she's unbuttoning your shirt, pulling it off, urging you back up onto the bed, removing your pants, socks, shoes. It's not long before you're as naked as she is, sucking on those nipples you'd wanted to touch, your hand buried between her wet thighs. Not long before you're hard again, your cock aching for something tight and wet. Not long before you're climbing on top of her, stretching her arms up above her head, pinning her wrists down, and sliding your cock deep into her cunt, fucking her slowly, inexorably, until she's moaning, arching up to meet your thrusts, pushing her wrists against your hands. But you don't let her go, you fuck her until she's sweating, twisting, screaming against you, coming around, and then you come again, you come hard, until your balls are emptied and there's absolutely nothing left to do but collapse, exhausted, against her.

Eventually, you roll over and pull her into your arms. You whisper in her ear, "Okay, okay. You can have an A. This time. But next week's assignment will be harder."

Wendy chuckles against your chest, and you give her a quick hug. Everything seems different somehow.

→

As you lie beside Wendy, resting, you can't help feeling that this is all rather strange. You don't know this woman at all, but you've done intimate things with each other's bodies, with each other's minds. You feel like there are some ways in which you do know her; you know what buttons you can push to make her react. And, of course, she knows the same about you. It's not romantic. Maybe it's friends.

It's past two A.M. If you want to get some sleep and be able to work tomorrow, you have to go. It's not easy leaving Wendy's agile, naked body in the bed, getting up and putting your clothes back on. But you're determined not to mess this up—you can have it all, a good career and lots of fun with her, though it's going to take willpower. And maybe going a bit short on sleep.

Wendy watches you dress, smiling contentedly. It's the first time you've really seen her smile. She looks . . . pleased. Satiated.

"We'll do this again?" you ask, pausing at the bedroom door.

Wendy shakes her head. For a minute, you think she's about to end things, call it all off. But then she says, "Not this. We won't do this again, but something else, something different, something interesting. If you can keep up with me." She grins at you, cheerfully wicked.

You grin back, happy to take up the challenge. "Oh, I think I can manage."

"Good. That's good." She closes her eyes and curls up in the tangled sheets. You've made a mess of the bed, but she looks beautiful in it.

"Good night, Wendy Lake," you say softly as you turn out the lights, close the bedroom door. She doesn't say good night back to you—she's asleep already.

THE END

"What?"

"It's a simple question, isn't it? Don't worry, I'm a med student, I'm over twenty-one, and you'll never have me in a class. Do you want one or not?"

Why not? "Um . . . sure."

She slides to her knees and, with quick hands, undoes your pants and pulls out your cock. The girl takes it in her mouth—she's wearing black lipstick, and it's oddly disconcerting, seeing a ring of black around your cock. But you can't worry about it for long, it feels too good, her small mouth moving on your dick, licking long lines down its length, sucking gently, then harder. Her hand comes up to circle the base, and she drizzles spit down until the base of your cock is coated, slick. Her hand moves quickly up and down the shaft while her mouth plays with the head, breathing lightly, then swallowing it down.

It's surreal, being there in the library stacks with the smell of old books filling your nostrils; you're standing in a shaft of winter sunlight, snow falling lazily outside, and you suddenly realize that is what you dreamed of when you were a young college student first pursuing the life of the mind, dreaming of being a professor someday. Old books and slender college girls, wet mouths and hard cocks moving blindly, faster and faster, in the library stacks. You're getting close, your hips fucking forward to meet her mouth, your hands coming down to her head—she shakes her head impatiently, and you let your hands drop to your sides. Whatever she wants, you'll take this as it comes. And she's going deeper now, taking your cock all the way down, and that's enough, that sends you coming, the jism rising . . . and just before you start to come, she slides out, and in one swift motion, grabs a book from the shelf and catches the come neatly in its open pages. When you're finished, she closes the book and puts it back on the shelf.

You know better than to question her about it, and honestly, you don't much care. It may be years before anyone opens that particular book. If not, well, they'll get an interesting surprise.

"Can I take you somewhere? Do something for you?" She intrigues you, this girl. You wouldn't mind seeing more of her.

"Sorry," she says, wiping her mouth dry. "I'm Catholic."

"What?"

"I'm going to stay a virgin until I get married. I admit, it's a technicality, but technicalities count. And sorry, Professor, I may have a thing for professors, but I'm not planning on marrying one. Thanks, though."

And she's gone, walking down the hall with her highlighted book. You wonder if she's planning on stealing it. You wouldn't be surprised.

THE END

This book was produced by Melcher Media, Inc.,
124 West 13th Street, New York, NY 10011. www.melcher.com

Charles Melcher / Publisher
Duncan Bock / Editor in Chief
Carolyn Clark / Publishing Manager
Andrea Hirsh / Director of Production
Megan Worman / Assistant Editor

Book design by Elizabeth Van Itallie
Cover photograph by Michael Cardacino/Photonica

Create Your Own Erotic Fantasy is based on an idea by Makoto Nakayama.

AUTHORS' ACKNOWLEDGMENTS
A nod to Professor Larry McCaffery . . . he knows why.—MH

Tours of New York, both real and virtual: Alex, Yuko. Modern Greek assistance: Asa, Nick. Comments on masculinity and critique of the manuscript: Andrea, David B., David H., Heather, Jed, Karen, Zak. Patience: Kevin, as always. This book is for Alex, whom I loved, and who has learned to love New York.—MAM

MELCHER MEDIA'S ACKNOWLEDGMENTS
Julia Gaviria, John Meils, Lauren Marino, Allison Murray, Ritsuko Okumura, Lia Ronnen, Mark Roy, Bill Shinker, E. Beth Thomas, and Amy Vinchesi.

MICHAEL HEMMINGSON is the author of *The Comfort of Women, Wild Turkey, The Dress, The Naughty Yard,* and *Minstrels*. He is the editor of *Wanderlust: Writers on Travel and Sex* and coeditor of *The Mammoth Book of Short Novels*. He lives in San Diego.

MARY ANNE MOHANRAJ is the author of *Torn Shapes of Desire,* editor of *Aqua Erotica* and *Wet: More Aqua Erotica,* and a consulting editor for *Herotica* 7. Her fiction has appeared in many anthologies and publications, including *Herotica 6, Best American Erotica 1999,* and *Best Women's Erotica 2000* and *2001*. Ms. Mohanraj lives in Chicago.